# MAKE
## IT
### count

## JESSIE HARPER

Cover Design: Y'all That Graphic

Editing: Librum Artis and Ryan Edits

Ebook ISBN: 978-1-955326-02-5

Print Book ISBN: 978-1-955326-03-2

✿ Created with Vellum

## ALSO BY JESSIE HARPER

### The Mint Springs Series

Make It Shine

Make It Burn

Make It Last

Make It Count

### The Finally Falling Series

Fight For It

Forget About It

Fix It

## ALSO BY JESSIE HARPER

### The Mint Springs Series

Make It Shine

Make It Burn

Make It Last

Make It Count

### The Finally Falling Series

Fight For It

Forget About It

Fix It

# 1

*Faith*

"You runnin' late this mornin'? That coffee's almost cold." Debbie points to the disposable cup on the diner counter.

"We added another delivery before yours. Are you setting your watch by when I get here every morning?" I grab the cup. "This is still plenty hot." My first sip still scalds my tongue.

"I was just wondering." Debbie thins her lips. As Ham & Eggs' oldest waitress—both in age and corporate longevity —she deals in small town gossip more than grits. Want to know the real dirt on someone? Debbie's usually got at least part of the story—which part is anybody's guess. Now I've gone and disappointed her by getting her expectations up and letting her down. She should know better; I'm not exactly Mint Springs' answer to Andy Cohen.

"Patty's getting fresh fruit from us at the bakery now." I hope that explanation gives Debbie something to chew on for a bit. The newest pastry at Patty Cakes isn't exactly hot gossip, but it might be better than nothing. "I hear she's thinking about fresh apple turnovers for the fall."

"You don't say?" Debbie cranes her gray head toward the stainless steel opening to the diner kitchen. "You hear that, Henry? Fresh apple turnovers." Henry only nods, still flipping bacon and sausage on the grill.

I've managed to beat the morning rush, but not by much. I'm going to have to start these deliveries even earlier if I want to get this produce out and be back in time to get started on the rest of my work. Vegetables don't tend themselves, and the hottest part of the day is no time to be out in the sun. These Georgia summers can be brutal, and I don't have time to chat the way Debbie's going to want me to.

"Well, I've got to get going. There's some extra kale in there today. Let me know if you'd like to try that out as a regular item."

"Kale?" Debbie wrinkles her nose. "You know Henry's not going to make anything with that."

"It's great for salads or sautéed. People might like it," I offer even though I know she's probably right. Still, I keep adding new items to people's produce orders in the hopes of finding converts to different fruits and vegetables. My father thinks it's a waste of time, but I'm determined to prove him wrong. If we want to keep growing Happy Trails into a bona fide supplier, we need to think outside the box.

Debbie shakes her head. "I'll see what Henry thinks, but don't get your hopes up. Where you off to now?"

"The Allens. I've got a delivery for the restaurant." I take another sip of my coffee to hide my smile. It's my last delivery of the day for a reason.

"Ah, going to see Charlie?" Debbie gives me a knowing look. "Nice to have him back in town permanently, isn't it?"

"It is." Although it's not what Debbie thinks. Charlie

Allen's been my best friend since elementary school. Kissing him holds all the appeal of licking a frog straight from the creek.

"Do I sense a little bit of a love connection?" Debbie leans on the counter, settling in for the kind of information she's been waiting for.

"With Charlie?" I stick my tongue out like a first grader. "Miss Debbie, I think your radar's way off on that one." I tilt my coffee cup toward her. "Thanks for the pick-me-up. I'll see you tomorrow." I wave to Henry and get another nod.

Debbie calls out after me as I push through the doors to the parking lot. "You mark my words, Faith Baker. You'll end up an Allen before it's all said and done."

The Allen farm isn't far from town and the drive's especially pretty. That's another reason to leave this delivery for last. I take my time on the back roads until I pull up to their new sign. I still can't believe Charlie and his brothers have moved back here for good and are making a go of starting a business. Or *businesses*, because what they've got planned is way more than some mom and pop thing. It's going to be a veritable empire once they're done.

I turn onto their property, gravel crunching under my tires. The place is really coming together. Chance—one of Charlie's older brothers—bought the family farm after their grandpa passed away. He's been running a design and remodeling business with his wife Lily. She's one of the main reasons he decided to stay in Mint Springs. He fell hard for her and moved into the old farmhouse. Their oldest brother Cooper has opened a distillery, and I drive by it on my way to Charlie's baby—the fancy new restaurant that's been his dream forever now. Charlie's younger brother is the one with the MBA, and Cade's been corralling the older three Allen boys as they try to make this all work.

Cade.

I nearly sigh as I pull my pickup truck into the lot in front of the restaurant. There's Debbie's gossip and the real reason I leave this delivery until the end. I've spent more summers than I can count stealing glances at Cade Allen. The boys lived in Nashville most of the year, but spent summers here with their grandfather and two unmarried aunts. They made the most of those summers, running around from sunup to sundown. That's how I ended up meeting Charlie and how we became fast friends. He'd never seen a girl who wasn't terrified of the giant worms he and his brothers dug up from around the river. Not only was seven-year-old me not scared, I showed him how to take one of those suckers and put it on a fishing hook. From then on we were inseparable, and I counted down the days every year until school let out and the Allen brothers showed up, dropped off by their father in a maneuver so fast he nearly left tire marks.

Their absentee father aside, the Allens turned out okay. What my father would call respectable. Trustworthy.

Handsome.

The word pops into my head as I put the truck in park. Cade's coming through the front door, distracted enough to almost collide with the front bumper of my truck. His hazel eyes raise to meet mine as he waves his hand in apology.

"Sorry, Faith."

I lean a bit out the open window. "No problem. Just watch where you're going. I'd hate to run you over on a day as nice as this." I give him a wide smile. I've been told it's one of my best features.

Cade is, as always, immune. "I'll be more careful." He's not even looking at me as he starts the walk back toward the distillery. His long legs eat up the space in front of him, and

I can't help but appreciate the way his backside fills out the pair of worn out jeans he's wearing.

Charlie would never let me live it down if he knew I'd been crushing on Cade for years. Sure, Cade had been a pest when we were kids, but the summer he showed up in Mint Springs with a broad set of shoulders and the kind of smoldering good looks only Brad Pitt would have been able to pull off, I noticed him for an entirely different reason than his ability to annoy the hell out of Charlie. Suddenly, right there in front of the Piggly Wiggly, Cade had become much, much more than Charlie's little brother.

Sadly, Cade hadn't seemed to recognize any kind of a transformation in me. Despite the automatic doors of the grocery store opening at the perfect time, accompanied by an almost cinematic rush of cold air, Cade's expression hadn't changed in the slightest. I blame that partly on the super-short pixie cut I was wearing. I'd never been one to waste much time on hair and make up, but, in that moment, I'd wished I had the kind of blonde waves my sisters spent hours perfecting. Maybe then Cade Allen would have noticed me. As it was, Charlie was shooing him away so we could get to the river to test out the new rope swing. Cade had come along anyway, the new-to-me muscles under his T-shirt on full display once we all stripped down to our swimsuits.

But that had been years ago. Now I'm a grown woman with no reason to pine after a man who doesn't notice I'm alive. And I have vegetables to deliver. No time to dwell on Cade Allen with lettuce wilting in the back of my truck. I grab the crate I packed for Charlie from the bed of the truck and march it into the restaurant, excited for him to see all the wonders I've grown with my own two hands.

"Charlie, wait until you see…" I put the crate down on the nearest table. No Charlie.

"He's in the office." It comes from the back of the building. The new chef the boys have hired waves me toward the office door with a flick of her wrist.

"Good morning, Jenna. I didn't see you back there." She and I haven't exactly become bosom buddies since she started working with Charlie.

"I'm testing recipes. I'm sure he'll interrupt whatever he's doing for you." I detect a hint of…sarcasm? Jealousy? Jenna keeps her dark head bent over whatever she's doing.

"Thanks." I don't try to force small talk with her. She hasn't been here long, but frosty is the nicest adjective I can come up with for her at the moment, and I like to be nice. I grab a mug from the space behind the bar and pour myself a cup of coffee. I think I hear Jenna huff, but I ignore it and give Charlie's office door the three raps that constitute our secret knock.

"Enter if you dare." Charlie's still eight years old sometimes.

I dare, of course, and walk into a giant mess. Charlie's got the place torn apart. "Remodeling?"

"Trying to set this space up for two. Jenna needs a desk in here." He stands with his hands on his hips, looking over the piles of papers and construction material. The building is new and parts of it are still unfinished. "I can fit two desks in here, right?"

"I brought you some new things to try." I'm not all that interested in Jenna's desk situation or the way Charlie bends over backward to accommodate her. Now who's jealous? That would be me.

"You did?" That's all it takes to get Charlie back from office planning into food. He does have a weakness, and I

love having someone to coo over my produce. Once he's seen the contents of the crate and given me sufficient kudos for the three varieties of eggplant and the perfection that is my Black Krim tomatoes, I'm in the best mood. I've gotten a viewing of Cade's butt and more praise than expected for my handiwork. I refill my mug and get ready to skip back out to my truck.

"You're going to have to start bringing one of those reusable coffee cups," Charlie chastises, but he isn't really angry. "You can't keep stealing all our mugs." I see Jenna's head lift a fraction. I can imagine she's not happy with my frequent pilfering of restaurant property.

"I always bring them back," I call over my shoulder. I'm momentarily blinded by the sun as I push through the front doors. It's why I completely miss the large obstacle now right outside the restaurant. The muscular object with the rock solid chest that I run into face first, dropping my mug of coffee onto the ground.

## 2

*Cade*

That'll teach me to look where I'm going. I avoided being hit by Faith's truck only to have an even worse encounter with her face pressed up against my chest. That is more touching than we've ever done and the only thing that kicks my brain into gear is the splash of hot coffee on my left foot. I've changed into shorts and a T-shirt to go for a trail run, and the scalding coffee is soaking through my sock. It's not a pleasant sensation, but it keeps the rest of me from having the reaction I would normally have to Faith Baker pressed tight against me.

Complete panic.

"Oh!" Faith falls, and I reach out to keep her from tumbling to the ground. It destabilizes me enough to topple us both in the end though, my butt hitting the gravel first and then my back. Faith comes down right on top of me.

*Focus on the foot. Focus on the foot.* My arms wrap instinctively around Faith's small torso and I find myself in a position I've imagined a million times but know I should never, ever have found myself in—Faith's entire body flush against mine. We both stare at each other for two beats before we scramble to our feet.

"I'm so sorry." Her cheeks are the color of the tomatoes she grows.

"No, that was my fault." I try to dust some of the dirt from my back. "You warned me earlier."

Faith grimaces. "Are you hurt? We fell pretty hard." Her hands come out to touch me but then pull away. She's like one of those puppets, with her strings keeping her just out of reach.

Falling hard is something I do all the time with Faith, not that I can tell her that. I try to erase the memory of her chest pressed to mine as I make sure I'm not too banged up. "I'm fine, I think, a little dusty is all."

"The coffee! Did that get you?" Faith's hands shoot out and again they pull back almost as quickly. It's like she's afraid to touch me almost as much as I am to have her do it.

"A little." I should have denied that outright, and I regret my decision to tell the truth immediately.

"Where?" Faith's eyes scan my body, looking for evidence, and I do my best to turn away from her under the guise of dusting myself off. These shorts are too thin to have Faith looking me over like that, especially when I can still feel the electricity from our earlier collision.

"It went... It doesn't matter. I'm fine." I make the mistake of looking at Faith directly. Her big blue eyes bore holes in me. "Are *you* hurt?" *Should have asked that right off the bat, genius.*

"You kind of broke my fall." Faith shoves her hands in the pockets of her overalls and rocks back a bit on her heels. "Sorry about that. Again. Sorry again." She shakes her head like she's clearing the cobwebs. "I should get going." She moves toward her truck but then turns and adds, "Nice *running* into you."

I know it's a joke, but I'm too stunned to laugh.

Faith gives an embarrassed lift of one shoulder and nearly flings herself in the cab of her truck, putting the thing in reverse before I can at least act like I have a sense of humor. I don't, really, but I could have tried to crack a smile, maybe. Too late now as I watch her drive away from me, a fool in my coffee-soaked sock, bits of gravel embedded in my elbows.

All worth it to have had those two seconds of Faith in my arms, even if I know it can never happen again.

"What are you frowning about?" My brother plops down next to me.

"I'm not frowning." I try to get the edges of my mouth to turn up a little to prove him wrong.

Charlie laughs. "Very convincing. Dinner's almost ready." He takes a sip from the glass of whiskey he's brought out with him. "Want a taste? It's the bottle Chance and Lily brought back from that last Nashville trip."

I take the glass from him and let the liquor burn my throat. It doesn't do a great job. That's the problem with my family's whiskey obsession: we've started drinking booze that goes down smooth enough to keep you from forgetting why you started drinking in the first place. "It's good."

"Good?" My pronouncement isn't convincing enough for Charlie. "It's a two-thousand-dollar-bottle. It had better be fantastic." He takes the glass back from me and takes another sip. "Do you get a little dried fruit?" He sniffs the liquor.

"Maybe." I'm not interested in dissecting the flavors in his drink. I'm still preoccupied with my literal run-in with Faith this morning. I'm a grown man. Why does she make me into a bumbling middle schooler?

"Remember how I told you I wanted to have Faith work on some garden beds out here?" Charlie looks out over the edge of my aunts' property. We eat dinner here most nights, sometimes with the entire family. Now that our two older brothers have wives of their own—lives of their own— they're here less and less.

"Yeah." I'm afraid to say much more. It's like thinking about Faith has made her the topic of conversation. When Charlie had initially told me he wanted her working out here on one of his restaurant projects, I'd had trouble keeping the surprise out of my voice. He wants us to grow some of the ingredients ourselves, and it makes sense. Faith is the person with the knowledge and expertise to make that happen. But Faith helping with Charlie's big idea means not just trying to avoid her when she stops by for deliveries or to see my brother socially, but for big chunks of time. Her cute little nose and that exuberant grin will be impossible to avoid if she's working here almost every day.

"Have we got money in the budget to get started on that this year? Small scale. We're too late for much more than herbs, probably. But we could do some cold weather vegetables. Experiment a little. Faith's on board if we decide to get started."

I could lie. My brothers trust me to watch the expenses, take care of the books. Charlie would never question me if I told him no. I could make him wait until next spring to start. By then maybe I'd manage to get this thing I've got for Faith under control. It's possible. I can hope so, at least, even if the past *twenty or so years* would be evidence to the contrary.

But lying's not in my nature—never has been—and the trust I've got right now with my family? I know how easily that can be broken. It's one of the reasons I keep my hands off Faith in the first place. Because I promised Charlie I would. Sure, we may have been kids, but she's as important to him now as she was to him then. I don't break promises, no matter how much I'd like to, and I don't lie to my brothers, especially not for something selfish.

"We've got enough for you to get started. Don't go crazy or anything, though. I can put together a firm number for you if you think you won't be able to resist burning through a wad of cash." There. I've counseled moderation. It's the best I can do to reduce the time I need to spend working hard at not staring at Faith.

Charlie slaps me on the back. "Thanks, Cade. It's going to be great. Trust me, we won't regret it."

Oh, brother, I'm already regretting it.

## 3

*Faith*

"Mama, do we need spoons?" My oldest sister's screeching for no reason. We all know *need* doesn't matter a hill of beans when you're setting the table for Sunday lunch. On Sundays we use the good china—my great-grandmother's set. The one with the tiny pink tea roses around the edges of the plates. One of my sisters will most likely inherit the dishes, though none of them will probably spend as much time getting the table perfect the way my mother does. Our weekly family lunch looks like something at the Ritz and that means spoons, obviously. All the silver comes out and the crystal, too. We may live on a farm, but on Sundays we have spotless white tablecloths and a spread to rival Buckingham Palace.

"Put them out," I hiss at Hope. "Don't make her justify it."

"But it's wasteful. We're not going to even use them." Hope starts to put them on the table anyway, along with the dessert spoons and cake forks. She's the last person who should be chastising anyone about wastefulness. I'd be willing to bet she's got on a brand new pair of shoes, ones she paid good money for but will only wear a few times. "And if you feel so strongly, you can be the one to polish them."

I'm on napkin duty, folding the crisp linen squares in half and positioning them next to the plates. I had once tried to fashion them into swans, but Mama hated that. She likes traditional—formal in a classic way. It's the way she likes the table set, the way she dresses, the way she speaks. It's the reason all the Baker girls participated in the debutante ball, the reason we all know there is no excuse to miss Sunday lunch, the reason I'm wearing a skirt even though I'd rather be in my overalls.

Constance breezes in with a basket full of yeast rolls. She's pulled her hair back in an elaborate updo, tiny tendrils of her long, blonde hair strategically escaping from the pile on top of her head. "Y'all better hurry up. Daddy's slicing the pork loin, and once it's ready he's going to want to eat."

Sunday might be the one day Mama goes all out, but for our father it's just another work day. That means I'll be working after we finish eating, too. A farm doesn't know to take a break for the weekend and, even though it's technically the Lord's day, try telling that to summer squash. Daddy can sit still long enough to eat and try to have pleasant conversation, but he can't fritter away an entire day. Neither can I. I'll be back in my overalls in a few hours.

I give the hem of my skirt a tug. It's shorter than I normally wear, and it's far from fancy. It hits me right at the knees and the top I've paired it with is barely more than a T-shirt. My sisters are much better equipped to dress the way my mother likes. When Charity makes her way into the dining room looking like a catalog model, I try not to frown. All three of my sisters are magazine perfect: clear blue eyes and long blonde hair, straight white teeth and tiny waists. Not a one of them can drive a tractor without hitting the fence, but none of that matters much. The older Baker girls weren't cut out for farm work. They were Homecoming queens, Junior Miss contestants, sorority chapter presidents. The kind of girls boys wanted to date and other girls wanted to be.

And then there was me.

Kickball champion and fastball thrower. More likely to be found down by the creek catching crawdads than trying out new hairstyles. Always running with the boys, not because I was hoping for kisses, but because I had plans to beat them in bike races. My mother had no idea what to do with me after three girly-girls. Luckily, my father didn't have the same problem.

That's how I became a certified daddy's girl. I tagged along on farm chores and learned how to hunt and fish. I may be a Goody Two-shoes when it comes to language, and I may come across as sweeter than sugar itself, but I'm deceptively tough. Most local boys know to give me a wide berth. I may be small, but I'm not dainty. Not by a long shot.

"Are we about ready?" My father's voice booms through the dining room. He does not like to wait for his supper. "Girls, help your mama get the rest of lunch out here." He's carrying a tray full of glistening sliced pork, and he winks at me when he puts it on the table. "Some of us have a full day still to put in."

"John, you can take a day to spend with your family." My mother's tone is more teasing than annoyed. This is the same dance we all do every Sunday. He'll sit through an hour and a half that could easily be condensed into twenty minutes, but he'll do it with a smile on his face because it puts a smile on Mama's face. That's what's important to my father. And she does the same for him, bringing him a beer and listening to bits of the Braves game on the radio he keeps out in the barn. She hates baseball, but she loves my father. He hates fancy dinners and clothes that need to be buttoned around your neck, but he knows it makes her happy when he makes an effort, so every week he puts on a starched shirt and plays nice.

Once Hope, Constance, and Charity are seated at the table, my father says grace. It isn't overtly religious. Despite my name, no one in our family puts much stock in religion. Mama named us all after virtues, but it seems we've all decided to prove those monikers wrong. Hope is the most pessimistic of us all; Connie can't be counted on for anything; and Charity wouldn't give you a nickel. She rarely even uses her full name these days, preferring to let her friends call her "Cherry," much to my mother's chagrin. We all might have been better off without such lofty goals to aspire to, being Jennifers or Annies or Lauras. But too late now.

"This is delicious, Mama." Hope always starts the compliments.

"It truly is. I always love your squash casserole." Connie slides a bite into her mouth and chews.

"Well, everything tastes better when you've grown it yourself, right, John?" My mother deftly deflects most comments that focus too much on her alone. She likes to give credit to Daddy and the hard work he puts in.

"I think so. I'm sure Faith agrees. The pork was even fed with some of last year's apples, although I'm not sure you can taste a difference." He cuts into the slice of pork on his plate and takes a bite. "Of course, your mother could make shoe leather taste delicious."

"Now, John." My mother blushes a little and ducks her

head, waving the compliment away. This is basically their answer to flirting, and it'll go on as long as we let it. My sisters tire of it early, and one of them usually changes the subject to something I find as exciting as watching paint dry. Today it's Charity who decides to go first.

"What do the dresses look like for Hadley's wedding?" She leans forward on her elbows even though that has the potential to get a swat from Mama.

"The dresses?" I take a sip of my sweet tea. "What do you mean?"

"Well, you're a bridesmaid, aren't you? Haven't y'all gone dress shopping? That wedding's coming up." Charity's determined nod is mimicked by my other sisters.

Frankly, I've been more concerned with the vegetable order I'll need to fill that day than with what I'm going to wear. I was surprised when Hadley had asked me to be in the wedding party, but she'd said she thought of me like a sister. Looking around this table, I'm not sure if I should have taken that as a compliment. Having Hadley marry Charlie's oldest brother is going to make her an Allen for real.

"We went. Hadley's dress is beautiful."

"We need more details than that. What does the neckline look like? Is there a train? Is it white or did she decide on ivory?" Hope's questions don't mean much to me.

"Um, it's white, I think. White-ish. It's long." No one is impressed with my description. Ask me to tell you the specifics of a certain kind of tomato and I can talk for hours. Ask me to describe a dress and I can barely give you the color.

"I'm sure she's going to look fantastic. She could wear a gunny sack and she'd still look great. And I'm sure that wedding is going to be absolutely perfect. Between her and

Lily they'll have style to spare." Connie sounds a little jeal-ous. "And getting to marry Cooper..." She puts a hand on her heart.

"He is hot." Charity's comment gets a sharp glance from Mama. "All those boys are. Always have been."

None of my sisters have managed to catch a husband yet and not from lack of trying. Two of Charlie's brothers are going to be off the market, and there isn't exactly a huge group of eligible men here in Mint Springs. When the Allens moved here, they were a welcome addition, according to my sisters. Then Chance married Lily and Cooper and Hadley decided to make it official. Now there are only two Allens left on the market.

"Is Hadley's dress...fitted?" We all know what my moth-er's asking. Hadley and Cooper put the cart ahead of the horse, but Mama can't bring herself to gossip. Even though we all know Hadley's expecting, Rose Baker will never come out and say that.

"It's a little loose. She's going in for another fitting the day before. She's been really sick so I'm not sure if she's going to be bigger or smaller." I hope that much information isn't too much. Mama likes to know things but nothing salacious.

"Poor thing. Those first months can be hard. Can you pass the rolls, please? And how about you tell us more about the dress you're going to be wearing?" Subject officially and masterfully changed, and I spend the next ten minutes sorely disappointing the table with my inability to adequately understand the difference between chiffon and satin.

"Blue's a nice color, but this whole wedding is going to be wasted on Faith," Hope offers. "She's going to be at the nicest event of the year, probably, and all she'll care about is the collard greens."

"The new chef's not going to do greens, I don't think." I ignore the eye rolls my sisters give me.

"That wasn't an open invitation to talk about vegetables, Faith. We want to know more about the important stuff— the interesting stuff." Charity tells me this like I'm hard of hearing.

"That is the interesting stuff," I protest.

I get a chorus of groans.

"Completely wasted," Hope grumbles, and I focus on my plate. If you ask me, I'm the one paying attention to the important things; it's my sisters who are focused on the wrong ones.

"I'm sure Faith will do her best to fill y'all in on all the details after the ceremony." My mother would probably like to know more about the guest list and the vows, too, but she knows this conversation isn't going to get any better for me. "Now y'all eat so your father can stop fidgeting from all this girl talk." She gives me a smile and a nod and the table falls silent again.

"*Oh*, did y'all hear about Charlotte Elkins?"

And my sisters are off again.

## 4

*Cade*

It always takes me a few minutes to muster up the energy to call my mother, and today's no different. I put it off as long as possible, coming up with plenty of things I need to get done before I dial her number. I spend an hour going over last week's numbers even though I've already combed through them twice. Once the laundry's all done and I've vacuumed the entire house, it's well past time. They'll be expecting me up at Sadie and Mae's for dinner in half an hour, so I won't have time for the conversation to drag on or get too deep, if I'm lucky, but I know my mother's lonely. And I owe it to her to at least check in.

She picks up on the third ring. She always picks up because she's always home. I'd love, just once, for her to be out living her life, too busy to take my call.

"Cade!" At least she sounds happy.

"Hi, Mama. How are you? Am I interrupting anything?"

"Of course not. I was watching a little TV." Whatever she was watching is still blaring in the background. "Let me turn it off."

Now there's nothing but the deafening silence of her apartment and the expectation that I'll fill it. "How was your week?"

"Good, good. I tried calling Cooper. I was going to let him know I'm coming for the wedding. I left him a message, but I know he's busy." She's letting him off the hook before she even hears his excuse. I'll need to remember to turn on the guilt with my oldest brother, make sure he returns that call.

"I'm sure it just slipped his mind to call you back. It's nice of you to come for the wedding, though. I wasn't expecting you to make the drive." She hates driving, especially at night, and she'd skipped Chance and Lily's wedding. I think that was less about the drive and more about the possibility my dad might make an appearance. Instead, neither of them had shown up. Chance had been disappointed, but not surprised. For our mother, forced time with our father is something to be avoided at all costs.

"Wouldn't miss it for the world. I let things get the better of me for Chance's. I'm not doing that ever again." Her determined voice is strong through the line, and I can imagine her face—pretty, though she always disagrees when anyone says that. In reality she's always been beautiful because she's my mother. Even when she's overcome with sadness, I can still see who she used to be.

"I'm glad to hear that, Mama. Nobody likes regrets." Myself included. Although my regrets are all still few and far between. My mother's regrets could fill the ocean and then some, and I'm always trying to make sure my brothers and I aren't included in that list. I know marrying our father is something she wishes she could undo or at least do differently. Their divorce was brutal, and she never really got back on her feet, never regained the feisty spark she used to be known for around here.

"You'd better be saving a dance for me, because I'm coming to celebrate." I can almost hear a smile there, and it makes me smile too.

"You know I will."

~

All through dinner, I stew. No one notices, of course, because I'm not exactly known for lighting up a room with my effervescent personality. My brothers joke and laugh, enjoying the chicken and dumplings my great-aunts have made this evening. I can barely taste anything, and when the lemon meringue pie gets carted out and my sister-in-law Lily starts to serve it, I can't hold my irritation in any more.

"Cooper, you need to call Mom."

He looks up from his pie and tilts his head to one side. I'm sure my request's coming out of left field; Cooper probably hasn't given any thought to the phone call or the message she left.

"She called you about the wedding. Left you a message."

"Mom called you?" Chance is more intrigued than anything. Admittedly, the rest of my brothers have little to no contact with either of our parents unless absolutely necessary. A gift on Mother's Day, maybe, or a call on her birthday is about as much as they can muster. I understand, but it still disappoints me. From where I'm standing, she did nothing wrong. Getting caught up in our father's drama shouldn't mean she gets cut out of their lives.

"Yeah." Cooper wipes his mouth with his napkin. "Last week. She's comin' to the wedding, I guess."

"Really?" Charlie asks in disbelief. "I wouldn't have expected that."

"Well, I'll believe it when I see it. There's still plenty of time for her to back out. Or she could not show up. That's a possibility too." Cooper shrugs. "We'll wait and see."

"She's coming. I talked to her today." I grip my fork tighter than necessary. "She's excited."

"That may be, Cade, but that doesn't mean she isn't going to wake up the day of the wedding and decide she's changed her mind." Cooper sighs. "She's done it before."

He's not wrong, but I hate that they all see her that way —unreliable and flighty, unconcerned with their feelings. They think she's selfish when she's anything but, and there's not a lot I can say to convince them otherwise.

"Did you give her a call today?" Mae's voice is less angry than the rest of the ones at the table. I nod and she gives my arm a pat. Mae and her sister Sadie have been refereeing our fights since we were little. They're the reason my brothers and I ate so well when we spent summers on this farm and the only voices of reason that can cut through the testosterone once things get heated.

"That's thoughtful of you, Cade. I know she appreciates it." Sadie gestures to my plate. "Taste that pie and let me know what you think."

"I'm hoping she can make it. I'd like to be able to spend a little more time with her." Hadley doesn't look at Cooper. "I think Lily'd like that too. It'd be nice to hear some stories about y'all growing up from your mother. Family's important."

That shames us all a little bit. We're fiercely protective of Mae and Sadie, and if you dare say a word about any of my brothers, you'd better be ready for a fist to the face. It's the same for Lily and Hadley now that they're family. The

Allens close ranks when an outsider makes trouble. It should be the same with our parents, but those wounds run deep.

"I'll call her tomorrow, how about that?" Cooper spoons more pie into his mouth. "But I'm not getting my heart set on her showing up for the wedding, and you shouldn't either." It's meant as much for me as it is for Hadley. "Manage your expectations."

"Way to bring us all down, Cade." Charlie rolls his eyes. "Can we get a little levity in here?"

"Serious isn't always all bad," Sadie admonishes.

"But does *he* always have to be so serious?" Charlie says it under his breath, but we all still hear it.

And I'm going to have trouble not taking it to heart. But later, when I'm elbow deep in suds, helping with the dinner dishes, Mae's comments help me feel a little better.

"You're a good son, Cade, and don't let your brothers convince you otherwise."

Easier said than done.

## 5

*Faith*

"What exactly are you trying to do over there?"

Charlie looks up from the new raised garden beds we've constructed, a smear of dirt across his face. "I'm looking at the edges of this thing. Are you sure this is deep enough?"

"Yes." With Charlie it's easiest to give a one word answer. My reminder of how we talked about all of this before is best left unsaid.

He gives me a half-hearted scowl. "Have you explained this to me before?"

"Yep." I hand him a basil plant, letting the leaves brush my fingers. I can't resist touching the herbs as we plant them, even if it makes me smell like a giant bowl of pesto.

"And I agreed to whatever's set up out here now?" Charlie pushes his spade into the soil.

"Yes." Charlie's had a lot on his mind. Opening the restaurant takes up most of his mental energy and the rest, I've come to realize, is taken up with the new chef. Jenna's giving Charlie fits at this point, although he'd never admit it.

I've seen the way he looks at her and know it can only mean one thing—Charlie's interested in more than her cooking.

"Well, at least I was smart enough to decide on this spot right here. It'll be nice to walk out the back door and be two steps from the herb garden."

"That's exactly what I told you." I hand him another plant.

"Figures it was your idea." Charlie wipes the back of this hand across his brow, smearing more dirt around.

"You sure you don't want me to do this part? I can knock it out in a few minutes." I'm a pro at getting plants into the ground lickity-split. I work for efficiency in the morning, trying to beat the heat and the sun, even though I do still love the feeling of both. I had let Charlie take over the planting in the hopes of being able to catch a glimpse of Cade, but so far, he's a no-show.

"I like doing it," Charlie confesses. "And it's giving me time with you. I haven't had enough of that lately."

I get that warm feeling in my chest that comes from the easiness of my friendship with Charlie. Now that he's in Mint Springs for good, I had thought I'd get more time with him. Growing up, we packed lifetimes into those summer days. Once August came, Charlie went home to Nashville, so there wasn't a minute to spare. We might not want to spend afternoons searching for crawdads in the creek anymore, but I thought having him here would be different. It turns out his schedule is pretty packed.

"Well, you're going to have to do it faster. You're giving me hives watching you pick along like that." I hand Charlie another plant. "Double time, Allen."

"You have someplace to be?" Charlie seems dubious about my social obligations.

"As a matter of fact, I do." He's not the only one with a

full schedule. "Aside from needing to get back to my farm, I've got a meeting of the Mint Springs Historical Society." I puff out my chest a bit. Although technically the meeting's just me and Molly Eagan, we're hoping to recruit a few more members.

"The what? Since when does Mint Springs have a historical society? And what in the world made you say yes to that?"

"Since two weeks ago. And I wanted to give back to the community. There are several places in town that might qualify for the National Register of Historic Places." Molly and I aren't one hundred percent sure about that last point, but Mint Springs is plenty old, and when Molly had asked me if I was interested in coming to a meeting, I'd reluctantly said yes. It's the kind of frou-frou thing I try to avoid usually. I'd even suggested she ask one of my sisters. The Historical Society would have been better suited to Constance or Hope or Charity; they all loved the debutante ball and cheerleading. They would probably love to flit around town doing "historical" things. But I was trying to expand my circle a little bit. This town is small, and I've exhausted all my normal avenues for meeting new people. There are only so many times you can enthusiastically introduce yourself to strangers over the hostas at Sullivan's Nursery. And I am running out of strangers.

When our first meeting at the library had turned out to be only me and Molly, there was no way I could make a graceful exit. The disappointment on Molly's face had been impossible to miss. Not a one of her country club friends had bothered to tell her they weren't coming. The plate of chocolate chip cookies and fifty copies of the meeting agenda told me she had expected a much larger turnout.

Instead she had me, stuffing my face with cookies and wondering what I'd gotten myself into.

"What do y'all do—this *society*?" Charlie's confused face peers at me over the first row of basil. "I've never even heard of it."

"It's new." I give him a wave of my hand, trying to make it sound like explaining more would take too long. "But I need to leave in twenty minutes. I don't want to be late."

"Fine. I'll finish this bed. Think you can get everything into that one over there?" There's a hint of challenge in Charlie's voice.

"In twenty minutes?" I try to act shocked. "That should leave me about ten minutes to spare."

I regret not going home to change as soon as I see Molly sitting in the back booth of Ham & Eggs. She's wearing one of those plaid sundresses, the tidy bows crisp and clean on her shoulders. She's taken off her pristine cardigan and draped it over her handbag sitting next to her. It matches, obviously. One sandaled foot peeks out from underneath the table, and I'd bet a hundred dollars the pedicure on her toes is new. She waves enthusiastically and smiles when she sees me, her red lips pulling away from her perfect teeth. I look down at my dusty overalls and work boots, certain I've got a few smears of dirt on me somewhere. But even if I'd gone back to my house and tried my best to look presentable, I would never come out looking as polished and shiny as Molly. Believe me, I've tried—and so have all three of my sisters. Connie, Hope, and Charity have all given me plenty of makeovers and wardrobe suggestions. None of it sticks.

Molly takes in my outfit. "Did you come straight from work?" Her nose wrinkles a bit.

"I had some work over at the Allen farm." I slide into the booth and grab a menu. I don't need it. The choices at Ham & Eggs have stayed the same for the last fifty years. But it gives me something to focus on other than Molly's perky nose.

"Ohhhh, with Charlie?" Molly leans across the table. "How's that going?"

"Fine. We're putting in some raised beds over at the restaurant. Herbs." I keep my eyes on the menu. I know that's not at all what Molly was talking about. She doesn't care about what I'm planting unless it's the seeds of a love affair with Charlie. The whole town's waiting to see when he and I will finally realize we were destined to be together. They're going to be waiting a long, long time.

Molly's mouth twists. "But you're spending time over there…"

"Well, I have to be there if those beds are going to thrive. Can't have it getting around that Happy Trails isn't reliable." I slap my menu down on the table, and Molly jumps. "I think I'm going to have a turkey club."

"Turkey club?" Debbie rescues me before Molly can ask any more questions. She scribbles my order down on her notepad even though she doesn't need to. Debbie's been waitressing at Ham & Eggs since before I was born. "And for you, Miss Molly?"

"A house salad. Italian dressing on the side, please." Molly touches her stomach reflexively. "And a glass of water with lemon." Molly's always been worried about her weight. She's got four of the cutest little kids you've ever seen, but even before babies she was worried about her middle. Baby fat is only cute on babies, apparently.

"I'm guessing you want sweet tea, Faith? And fries." Debbie gives me a big smile. She knows I'm never going to turn down french fries.

"Yes, ma'am." Molly's like my sisters—always trying to cut calories—but I'll have all this worked off well before dinner.

"And what are you two over here scheming about?" Debbie looks at the stack of papers Molly's got in the middle of the table.

"We're starting an historical society for Mint Springs," Molly announces far too loudly and proudly.

"Well, I'll be. Historical, you say?" Debbie leans over me a bit to get a better look at the flyer Molly's handing her.

"Yes. And I was just about to tell Faith about our first big challenge." Molly squares her shoulders.

"Challenge?" I do not like the sound of that.

"Yes. Faith and I"—Molly corrects herself—"the Mint Springs Historical Society, I mean, is going to save the old mill."

# 6

*Faith*

"The mill? Mint Springs has a mill?"

"That's exactly what I said! It's over on River Road, apparently. Want to take a drive with me after we finish here and check it out?" I'd love to get Charlie's thoughts on Molly's "Save the Mill" campaign.

"Can't. I've got to check in with Jenna about the wedding menu." Charlie's suddenly very interested in the seed catalogs I've brought over.

I try not to read too much into Charlie's unavailability. Work is important, and this foray into saving some place I've never heard of is more Molly's baby than mine. "They want to tear it down to build condos or something. Molly's convinced we can cobble together enough of a plan to stall things until we can come up with the money ourselves."

"And then do what? If no one's used the place in years, then I think it's obvious there's no real untapped market for milling things. Is that even right? Do you mill things?" Charlie scratches his chin. "See? I don't even know what verb to use. That's how much I need a mill around here."

"That's why I wanted to go and see it for myself. Molly said it hasn't been operational for thirty years, but it used to be kind of a community hub. And it's a part of *history*, Charlie. Mint Springs history." I say this like it legitimizes everything. "I'm going to do more research tonight, but the stuff she's found already is fascinating."

"Uh-oh." He cocks his head to the side.

"Uh-oh, what?" I sit up a little straighter, unsure about this concern Charlie's showing all of a sudden.

"I can already see it happening. You're getting attached. I can hear it in your voice. And you're doing that thing."

"What thing?"

"That thing you do with your fingers when you're excited. Pulling on them." Charlie looks at my hands.

I make my left hand release the fingers of my right. "Of course I'm excited. It's interesting, Charlie, and I get to..." Do what, exactly, I'm not sure. "I get to be part of it."

"But you're already part of some pretty big things. This doesn't sound like a small project."

"It isn't even a project yet. I'd have to figure out how we'd even get started. We'd have to figure out how to finance the thing, if the building's even salvageable." It's already starting to feel daunting and I'm just at the starting line, but I've also got a feeling building in my chest, one I haven't felt in a while other than when I get the occasional glimpse of Cade.

*Excitement.*

"You know who you should talk to about this?" Charlie's already back to thumbing through the catalog in front of him.

"Who?" I lean forward on my bar stool.

"Sadie and Mae. If the mill was anything special, they'll know. And they'll know other people you could talk to about it." Charlie flips a page. "It might help with your *research*."

"That's a great idea." I try belatedly to temper my enthusiasm and Charlie lifts an eyebrow. "I'll definitely talk to them." Charlie's great-aunts have lived in Mint Springs their entire lives. I don't know why I didn't think to ask them about the mill first.

"And you should talk to Cade." This time when Charlie doesn't look up, I'm relieved. The mention of his brother's name makes it hard to keep my face business-like.

"Cade?" I squeak out. *Very cool, Faith.* "Why?"

"Well, aside from being a genius with money, he interned at a nonprofit when he was working on his MBA. He'd know about grants and things like that." Charlie's head snaps up from the glossy pages in front of him. "You can ask him about it tonight at the bachelorette party. You're coming to that, right?"

"*I* am, but why would Cade?" By definition this party is supposed to be ladies only, and I hadn't factored hours in the presence of the youngest Allen into the equation when I'd told Hadley I'd attend.

"We're combining Cooper's bachelor party with Hadley's hen party. Thought it'd be more fun that way." Charlie gives me an encouraging smile and I try to give him one back, even though trying to keep from making an idiot of myself in front of Cade is the least fun thing I can think of right now. I'm already a dork in social situations, and this one suddenly got decidedly more social.

"Are Sadie and Mae home now, do you think?" I'm already itching to get off of this stool and away from the idea of asking Cade anything.

"Probably. Why don't you go over there and find out?"

"Cutter's Mill? I haven't thought about that place in years." Mae looks at Sadie. "Remember the general store?"

"Of course. That was about the only thing left back when we would take a trip over there. But Daddy used to tell us it had been a big deal to bring your corn to the gristmill. Around here it was one of the only places to see all your neighbors. They'd do a little shopping, maybe fish in the water there. People would line up to wait their turn with their corn. Then, when they added the sawmill and cotton gin, it was even more popular. The boards from our barn were actually milled over at Cutter's." Sadie taps her chin, thinking. "When we would go, it wasn't quite like that, but it operated until the 1960s."

"In the Civil War, both the Union and Confederate sides used it," Mae offers, her gray head bobbing. "Of course, you won't find anyone who remembers that first-hand."

"Is it even still standing?" Sadie asks in disbelief. "It's set back from the road enough that you can't see it unless you're looking."

"Molly and I are going over tomorrow. It sounds like it might be a piece of history worth saving." What we'd do with it I have no idea, but I try to keep a little positivity in my voice.

"Well, if anyone can do it, it's you and Molly. I wouldn't want to get in the way of either of you girls." Mae gives my arm a pat. "Now, I think we all need to get a move on so we can look beautiful for Hadley's party."

No amount of primping is going to make me look like the other girls. I'm not sophisticated or sexy. "I was planning on going like this."

Sadie and Mae take one look at my work overalls and

both gasp. Sadie even goes so far as to bring one dramatic hand to her chest.

"Oh, no, Faith." Mae vigorously shakes her head. "We won't keep you any longer. You head straight home and get to work. Wear something that makes you feel pretty. Show off that cute figure of yours."

"And with a face like that? You hardly need anything else. A little mascara. Some lip gloss. You'll have all those boys eating out of your hand." Sadie gives me a wink as she shoos me out onto the front porch.

"If you say so..." I barely get the words out before the door closes behind me. If I wasn't dreading this party before, I am now.

## 7

*Cade*

"I still don't understand why we have parties like this. And for Hadley? She's not going to enjoy herself."

Charlie shoots me a look. "We aren't forcing them to have a party, Cade. They wanted to do this. You don't have to stay all night; once everyone's seen your *happy, smiling face*, you can go back to your spreadsheets or whatever you do for fun on a Friday night." He tips back his glass, emptying it. "You want another drink? Maybe that'll loosen you up a bit."

"I'm still working on this one." No need to get plastered. I'll probably have to make sure everyone gets home safe, anyway. Can't exactly be the designated driver if I'm throwing back drinks all night. "There aren't going to be strippers, are there?" I look around our distillery and start thinking about all the things I should move out of harm's way. Cooper won't appreciate things being broken even if it is technically his party.

Charlie tilts his head back and laughs loud and long. "No, little brother, there aren't going to be any strippers.

Although, now that I think about it, it would have been worth it to get a few so we could all watch your horrified reaction."

"I wouldn't have been horrified," I argue. "I just know it might make some people uncomfortable. And I know no one here would tip worth a shit."

Again Charlie laughs. "If the day ever comes when I need to hire a stripper for a bachelor party, I'll be sure to put you in charge of fair compensation for the performers. Can you at least try to pretend like you're having a good time?" He slaps me on the back. "Try getting the corners of your mouth to move a little. That's called a smile, Cade. No one wants you to frown all night."

"I wasn't frown—" But it's no use. Charlie has moved on. I try to make my face do something other than grimace. I'm working on looking the tiniest bit more relaxed when she walks in the door. Faith always manages to take my breath away, but tonight she damn near makes my heart stop. She comes through the front door of the distillery wearing a pair of jeans that leave nothing to the imagination, her hair in waves that fall down to her shoulders. When she scans the room, I quickly look away. There's no telling what my face will give away if I make eye contact with her.

"Faith!" Charlie welcomes her in as soon as he sees her. "Whoa. You look..." He leans back so he can dramatically take her in from head to toe.

Pink creeps up Faith's neck and her cheeks redden a touch. "It's too much, isn't it?" she asks, before she ducks her head.

If you ask me, it isn't nearly enough. Faith kills me on the daily with her overalls and work boots, seeing her in something else tonight has me thinking all sorts of thoughts

I shouldn't. But she isn't asking me, she's asking Charlie. And so instead of telling her she looks like an angel dropped straight from heaven the way a man should, he teases her.

"What's the occasion? You lookin' to get lucky?"

The redness on Faith's cheeks deepens. "Sadie and Mae suggested... They told me..." Even her stammering is cute, although I would like to murder my brother for making her do it in the first place.

"Settle down." Charlie wraps her in a hug that has my jealousy surging. "You look great." It's not the adjective I would have used, but at least it gets Faith smiling.

"Thank you." She tucks a strand of hair behind her ear as Charlie makes space at the bar and works on getting her a drink. Faith isn't much of a drinker, but she takes the glass he offers her. The staff has mixed up some specialty drinks using the liquor my brother Cooper makes here, and all the ladies are drinking something called a Hanky Panky. I'm a beer or bourbon man myself, but from the way everyone is sucking down those drinks, I'm guessing they must be sweet. That's a quality that usually means trouble.

I see Faith finish three drinks before we decide to move the party to Bootlegger, Mint Springs' only bar. It's a certified hole-in-the-wall, but we've been going there since before we should have been, and it's the only place in town where people can get a little rowdy. I consider asking Faith if she wants to ride with me, I'm sober as a judge and not so sure about everyone else. I haven't been watching anyone the way I've been watching her. She hasn't noticed, of course, mainly because I haven't said a word to her all night.

"Are you going out with the rest of the young people?" My aunt Sadie asks me, coming up beside me and giving my arm a squeeze. "Might be nice to cut loose a little."

"I'm not really planning on doing much of that." I give

my great-aunt a small smile. "But I'll probably go." I search the room for Faith. "Somebody has to make sure everyone gets home safe."

Sadie's eyes follow mine. "Yes, please make sure *everyone* gets home." She gives my chest a pat. "Faith came over to see us this afternoon."

"She did, did she?" I feign disinterest.

"She's got a new project she was telling us all about. Saving the old mill. You should ask her about it."

"What mill?" I look down at my geriatric aunt, but she's already moving away, her arm waving as she goes. "Ask her yourself, Cade. It'll be a good conversation starter."

"I don't need a—" *What does she think I am, an imbecile?*

But it's the first thing I do when we get to the bar—I seek out Faith and prepare to have a conversation. My palms are sweating enough to have me thanking the dive bar gods that the beer in my hand is ice cold. I shift it back and forth as I wait for an opportunity to mention my new information to Faith.

"I hear you've got some kind of project going."

She doesn't hear me, already in an animated discussion with my sister-in-law, Lily. I clear my throat and get a raised eyebrow from my brother's wife. Normally I'd try to include Lily in the conversation, but right now I'm wishing I had some kind of excuse to get her moving along. I stand there shifting from one foot to the other until Lily takes pity on me.

Lily gives me a smirk. "I should probably go and check on your brother." The way she saunters off lets me know she'll be reporting all this back to Chance. Hell, she'll probably tell Cooper and Hadley too. Nothing like a little family gossip to liven up a Friday night.

"I heard you have some kind of new project?" I have to

shout it over the twanging of Florida Georgia Line from the jukebox. I lean closer to Faith to be sure she can hear.

"What?" Her lips are pink and full. They get too close to my ear when she moves toward me.

"Your new project," I shout and finally get a nod.

"I told Charlie you don't need to help me with it, but I appreciate you doing it. I was going to talk to you myself." Faith's lips brush my ear, and her hand lands on my chest.

"I'm helping you?"

"Yes, thank you." Apparently, Faith didn't hear that the way I intended and apparently my brother's taken the liberty of telling Faith I was available for whatever she's got planned.

This is getting ridiculous. Whatever Charlie's volunteered me for, he hasn't said boo to me about it. I should be getting annoyed. I've got plenty on my plate without adding this thing Faith's doing to the pile. But it's *Faith's* thing and that's what keeps me over in this corner of the bar getting closer and closer to her until we're only inches apart, putting together the pieces as best I can.

Predictably, a fight breaks out on the other side of Bootlegger. Every Friday and Saturday night someone in this bar says something untoward about someone else's mother. As the fists start to fly, I instinctively put my arm around Faith and move her toward the front door. The rest of our party's headed that way. None of us want to get sucked into something that's none of our business.

Out in the parking lot, it becomes clear several of us have been overserved—Faith included. She sways a little bit from side to side as we wait for the stragglers to emerge from the building.

"Shit." Chance's shoulders slump. "I left my tab open."

It turns out everyone did, and all faces turn to look at

me. "I'll take care of it." I trot back to the bar and make sure all the drinks get paid for. I leave a generous tip because working at Bootlegger seems like a grind, especially if you have to clean up broken bottles after every shift.

I come back out to a nearly empty parking lot. Even my car is gone, probably commandeered by one of my brothers who has no business driving it. I catch a glimpse of Charlie walking ahead of me, Faith on one side and our new chef for the restaurant on the other. That lucky bastard has managed to end up with two of the finest ladies from our group and I'm sure he hasn't even noticed. I can say that with absolute certainty about Faith. Charlie looks right through her. They may be best friends, but I'll never be able to understand why he doesn't see her the way I do, the way I can't stop myself from seeing her.

"Hey, wait!" I have to break into a jog to catch them. "Were y'all really going to leave me here? After I settled up for everyone?"

Charlie looks relieved to see me. He's even more relieved when I volunteer to take Faith home once we get back to the farm. She's in no shape to drive. My car's back in the distillery parking lot, thankfully, and we have a time loading her into the passenger seat. She'd fallen asleep with her head on my shoulder in the backseat of Charlie's car, and I'd let her stay that way as long as possible. Now she's awake again, but making zero sense as she lectures me while I drive.

"It's because you're the smart one, Cade. The smartest." Faith punctuates each word with a finger jab in the air. "And Jenna." She blows an exceptionally spitty raspberry, then reaches over and grabs my thigh. I nearly launch myself out the front windshield.

"Are you feeling okay over there? Should I roll down

your window?" I do not want Faith to throw up in my car. I try to concentrate on the road, but she's distracting, and her hand has stayed on my leg.

"And the handsome one. The handsomest. Most handsome. Out of all those boys." Faith's fingers flex on my thigh, making me hit the gas pedal harder than necessary a few times. "Pull over."

The lurching can't have been great for her stomach. "Right now?" I swerve a little on the country road, aiming the car for the side. Once I have the car stopped, I expect Faith to bolt from her seat and out into the grass near the ditch. Instead, she stays right where she is and swivels to face me. Her face is illuminated in the moonlight, her mouth set in a determined line.

"So now you know," she announces.

"Know what? Do you need to get out?" I start to open my door.

Faith's hand tightens on my leg. Her eyes are glassy from all the alcohol. "What I just said, Cade. I know I'm not Jenna. I don't have that crazy sexy thing going on. Emphasis on the crazy, I think, personally. And I don't have the easy sexy thing Lily pulls off. I don't even have the Daisy Duke sexy thing Hadley manages to make look appealing when it maybe shouldn't be." Faith takes my hand. "But I have my own thing. And you have your smart, handsome thing. You understand, right? You know what I'm saying."

I have no idea what Faith is saying. Between the slurring and the disconnected thoughts, I'm not sure of much of anything except that she's touching me in more than one place which is two more places than she usually does. I try to think of something to say to get to the bottom of things, but my mouth just hangs open like an idiot.

Faith lets out a frustrated breath. "Fine, if you won't do it, then I have to."

And then she leans forward and plants one on me.

## 8

*Faith*

*Ouch.*

That's about the only thought I can get out this morning. I groan in a way I haven't since I pulled a muscle in my back last summer when I tried to plant all the tomato seedlings myself. This isn't that kind of pain, though. Last year's injury was the result of hard work. Today's is all about dumb choices. I got all dressed up to make a drunken fool of myself.

At least that's what I think *might* have happened. The details are fuzzy, but I have one of those warning feelings in my belly, the kind that keeps a muscle memory of wrongs even if you can't remember them. I'm hoping I didn't blurt out how I feel about Charlie's new hire. I hadn't expected Jenna to be at Hadley's party last night and hadn't expected her to basically growl at me all evening. What was that all about?

I roll on my side and my stomach sloshes a bit. *Ugh*. There's a reason I don't drink much, and this feeling is it. I give myself a second to pull things together—deep breath, feet on the wooden floor next to my bed, eyes closed for two beats. Once I'm good enough to stand, I take in the outfit I'm wearing. It's the one from the night before, and that cannot be a good thing. I have a vague memory of leaving Bootlegger and getting in Charlie's car, but that's about all of it.

My foot bumps up against the trash can from my kitchen. *How in the heck did that get in here?* Even not remembering a thing, I know I wouldn't have drug that all the way into my bedroom. There's also a glass of water on my bedside table, and, come to think of it, it's awfully dark in here for what I'm pretty sure is well past sunup. Yep, my blinds are closed tight when I normally leave them open. I get up before the sun on most days, so keeping light out isn't one of my concerns.

I get that tingle of dread in my belly again. I'm now almost one hundred percent sure I'm about to have a thorough teasing from Charlie Allen. It has been years since I got even a little tipsy, and there's no way he'll be able to let last night fade into obscurity. Nope. This will give him hours of material to torture me with—days maybe. I'm half expecting to find him in the living room when I make it all the way down to the end of the hall. He'll be waiting on the couch, already more than happy to start ribbing me. But it isn't Charlie in my living room.

It's Cade.

He's got his boots off and is stretched out on my loveseat with his hands behind his head. Although stretched isn't the right word exactly; his legs hang off one side at the knees and his feet dangle there like vines from a tree. The angle of his head looks so uncomfortable that my own hand comes up to rub my perfectly healthy neck. If he's been here all night, he's going to need a visit to the chiropractor. Still, his face looks relaxed, happy even. I let myself stare longer than

I should, pretending I'm not taking advantage. His mouth twitches and then his eyes fly open like he can feel the weight of my gaze drilling into him.

"Oh." The word comes out in a rush as he struggles to sit up. "I didn't mean to fall asleep. I wanted to make sure you didn't need anything and I must have..." A goofy smile tugs at the corners of his mouth. "How are you feeling?"

"Good. Fine. Did you drive me home?" He must have if he's here now, but none of that makes sense. Why would Cade have driven me and not Charlie? Why wouldn't Charlie have taken me to his house instead of making his brother drive me all the way back here? He's got a guest room. He couldn't put his best friend in it after she'd had too much to drink?

"Yeah." Cade's brow creases. "Of course I did."

"Why didn't I stay at Charlie's?"

"He was dealing with something with Jenna. Don't you remember?" Cade looks a little bit green. Maybe he's as hungover as I am this morning.

"Not really. I remember getting in Charlie's car to come back from Bootlegger, but the rest of the night is mostly a blur. I'm sorry you got stuck with me." I shrug, but Cade doesn't look angry. He blinks a few times, shaking his head a little.

"I wasn't upset about bringing you home. I... You really don't remember anything about the ride here?" His voice has this pleading note in it, one I've never heard from Cade before.

"Should I make coffee? I think we could both use a cup." I'm not sure what to do with Cade in my house and reverting to my manners seems like a good way to mask all of that.

"Sure, I guess." Cade stands, fishing around for his

boots. "Then I can take you to get your car." He stands, suddenly too big for my house, taking up all the space with those broad shoulders and long legs. He's back to smiling now, at least, even if it looks a little forced.

I scurry toward the kitchen and try to remember how to make coffee. I seldom have men in my house, and this one in particular is throwing me into a tizzy. When Cade materializes in the kitchen doorway, I nearly drop the entire bag of coffee grounds onto the floor. The scoop clatters on the tile, and he bends down to pick it up.

"Need any help?"

I'm sure it looks like I need all the help I can get right now. "I've got it. Just a little butterfingers is all." I lift one shoulder. Good Lord, I'm acting like one of those ditzy girls you see on the kind of television shows my sisters watch.

"Let me know if you change your mind. We could also stop for coffee at Ham & Eggs on the way back, if that's easier. I could buy you breakfast." Cade's looking at me like he's not sure if I bite. Since everyone in town knows I absolutely do not, I can only assume that's another side effect of last night's gin.

"You don't have to do that—oh, dang it!" I make my transformation into a sitcom heroine complete with a smack to the forehead. "I'm supposed to meet Molly this morning to work on Historical Society stuff. Can you drop me at the diner? I'll see if I can get her to bring me by the distillery to get my car."

"I can take you. That's the new project you've got going, right? Aren't I supposed to be helping out with that?" He looks me up and down and my skin heats. "But you should probably take five minutes to change. Don't want the whole town talking about you turning up for waffles in last night's party clothes."

I know Cade means it as a joke, but I'm sure no one would blink if I wore this outfit for a week. Despite Charlie's teasing reaction yesterday, the clothes I choose to wear go mostly unnoticed around here. Not that I'm going to tell Cade that, though. If he thinks me showing up in last night's outfit would cause a stir, then I'm going to let him keep thinking that.

"Good idea. Give me a second and we can go."

Cade moves a little to let me pass, but I can still get a lung full of him as we negotiate the doorway. He smells a little like Charlie—all the Allen boys seem to still use the same brand of soap—but there's something there I can't quite put my finger on. Something almost chocolatey that's all Cade. I keep myself from licking him to find out if he tastes the same as he smells. I imagine being bold enough to do a thing like that, stopping in front of him and rising up on my tiptoes, running my tongue up the section of his neck I can reach that way. He'd be surprised for sure and probably a little horrified. Nope. There's no way I'm doing anything like that with Cade Allen.

No matter how much I might like to.

## 9

*Cade*

She doesn't remember. Either that or Faith Baker is a much better actress than anyone's ever suspected. Oscar-worthy. I had expected a little embarrassment this morning, maybe. Last night was a little out of character for her and definitely not the way she normally acts with me. Faith may be forthright with Charlie, but with me she keeps her cards close to the vest. She certainly isn't one for drunken late-night confessions.

But last night she was.

And, boy, was she a talker. She was spilling plenty of secrets and most of them were about me. The anecdote about my brother crapping his pants in tenth grade because he couldn't make it back home and didn't want to have to go at the movie theater was just icing on the cake. I'll keep that one in my back pocket for the next time Charlie needs a little putting in his place. But the rest? That's for me alone.

Especially the kiss.

Because when Faith had kissed me last night, I had kissed her back. She'd startled me when she'd leaned over the center console and mashed her face against mine. Maybe it wasn't the sexiest first kiss ever, but that hadn't mattered one bit to me in the moment. I didn't let it get any further than that; I'd have been a fool to let it turn into more, knowing how much she'd had to drink. I'd wanted to, but knew she might regret it in the morning. And I'd had to consider if it was worth the punch in the mouth I was going to get as soon as my brother found out about it. That calculation had been easy to make. Letting Faith press her lips against mine was worth anything my brother might try to dish out. I was more than willing to pay that price. And I had been looking forward to trying it again this morning. Turns out she doesn't even remember doing it.

Driving with her now, I have trouble keeping my eyes on the road. Faith is in a T-shirt and jeans, her hair pulled back in a ponytail. But it doesn't matter what she's wearing. The little spray of freckles she's got along the bridge of her nose is even cuter in the morning, and the way she huffed a bit when I'd opened the car door for her had me biting back a smile. Right now I'd like the chance to pull this car over again and memorize everything about her.

She huffs again when I move in front of her to open the door to the diner. Plenty of heads turn, and my hand comes out to rest on the small of her back. Faith jumps a little and her eyes go wide.

"I can get myself through a doorway," she whispers. Her eyes shoot down to my hand, and I make sure it stays at my side.

"Just opening the door." That's not entirely true. I've spent a lifetime not touching Faith, and now I can't seem to stop myself from doing it.

Molly's sitting in a back booth, and the flicker of surprise that moves across her face quickly morphs into a smile. She waves us toward her, and I brace myself for what's sure to be twenty questions.

"Well, good morning. I wasn't expecting an extra guest. Luckily, I got us a booth." Molly looks me up and down, my wrinkled shirt and last night's pants not going unnoticed. "*This* isn't the brother I normally expect to see you with, Faith." It's less of a question and more of an invitation to tell her everything. Gossip in this town's worth more than gold, and right now Molly Eagan's sitting on the jackpot. Or so she hopes, at least, if the tilt of her bright red mouth is any indication.

"Cade's offered to help us with our project." Faith slides into the booth, and I debate whether or not she intends for me to slide in next to her.

"He's joining the Historical Society?" Molly screeches it loud enough for the entire restaurant to hear.

"The what?" I hurriedly plop down next to Faith, our thighs touching in the too-small space.

"The Mint Springs Historical Society," Molly clarifies. "We're currently in a fight to save Cutter's Mill."

I look at Faith. "A fight?" I didn't even know Mint Springs had a mill.

"Well, not a fight so much as a quest. A mission, maybe? We haven't worked out the details yet." Molly gives me a blinding smile. "I had no idea you were interested in the town's history, Cade."

"Well, I'm...uh." The history of Mint Springs has never crossed my mind. Not even once.

"Cade knows a lot about nonprofits. He worked for one when he was finishing his MBA. Where is Debbie? I could use some coffee." Faith scans the busy restaurant for its most senior waitress.

"That's going to be useful. We're brand new and haven't

set up any of the business end of things. You'll be invaluable for that." Molly gives me another smile and reaches out to pat my arm. I can see how she manages to charm people around here into doing her bidding. I can easily imagine her cajoling me into buying something at a bake sale or walking away from the Christmas bazaar with an armload of those monogrammed T-shirts she sells. Her business has some kind of cutesy name I can never remember, but I'm not about to confess that now.

"I'll help however I can." I cut my eyes toward fidgeting Faith. "You really need that coffee, don't you?" I raise my hand in the air and try to get Debbie's attention.

"That and a glass of water would go a long way toward making this morning better." Faith blows out a breath. "I'm never drinking again."

"You two tie one on last night?" Molly fishes. "I heard y'all were out at Bootlegger."

"Everyone was out at Bootlegger," I confirm. "But Faith here did have maybe one drink too many. We were celebrating Hadley and Cooper. The wedding's coming up."

"And no one is happier for them than me and Brad," Molly gushes. "Hadley and Brad used to date." She whispers it conspiratorially, but I don't need the reminder. Molly's husband lost out to the magic that is my brother Cooper. Not that Molly isn't a fine choice, and they've got a house full of freckle-faced kids to show for it. Still, Molly likes being able to tell everyone that Brad Eagan chose her over Hadley. Small town stuff for sure.

Finally Debbie makes her way to our table, hot pot of coffee already in her hand. "Sorry to keep you waiting, this place is a zoo this morning." She takes one look at Faith and fills her cup to the brim. "Rough morning, Faith?"

"Too much fun at Hadley's bachelorette." Molly leans

toward Debbie like she's sharing a secret. "But she's still here for a meeting of the Historical Society."

Debbie fills my cup. "Y'all roped Cade into this too?"

"It's not too late for you to join, Debbie. I'm sure we could use your talents on this mill project." Molly clasps her hands together in front of her.

"Doubt I'd have the time for that. Sounds like you folks have some pretty big plans." Debbie shakes her head.

"We do?" I wasn't banking on this taking up huge chunks of time.

"I'll fill you in on everything in a minute, silly. Wait until you hear what Faith and I have in the works." Molly busies herself with her menu while I try to get a look at Faith.

She's sipping on her coffee like it's the only thing standing between her and damnation, her hands wrapped tightly around the mug. I'm hoping she'll find her tongue here in a minute and let me know exactly what I've signed up for. She lets out a sigh and takes another sip. I desperately want to be able to reach out and touch her, but I know I'll never hear the end of that. Besides, as far as Faith's concerned, we're exactly where we were yesterday. She's my brother's best friend, and I'm some twerp who's been following them around for years. Only now I know that's not the whole story. Not at all. And now I've kissed her, even though I know I wasn't supposed to.

And I'd like to do it again.

## 10

*Faith*

"I heard something *fascinating* yesterday."

That is never how you want to start Sunday lunch at the Baker house. At least, it's never how *I* want to start. My sisters, on the other hand, are all ears when it comes to introductions like that.

"Fascinating?" Connie drags the word out until it's almost unrecognizable. "Is it the same thing I heard, do you think?"

"I'm thinking it might be," Hope teases. "Does it have to do with a certain sister at this table? One who might have forgotten to mention something about having breakfast at Ham & Eggs with someone interesting?"

"Well, it isn't me." Charity's fork stops just shy of her mouth. "And I have no idea what either of you is talking about." She takes the bite of her chicken salad and chews, waiting for someone to clue her in.

I keep my eyes on my plate, hoping beyond hope that my sisters aren't talking about what I think they are. My mother's chicken salad is delicious, but I don't dare take a bite right before I have to defend myself against the probing questions my family will have about Cade.

"Faith? Anything you want to tell us?" Connie's smile is full of mischief, the kind that usually results in jokes at my expense.

"I joined the Mint Springs Historical Society. I'm a founding member." I get some strawberry salad on my fork and take my time chewing.

"That's lovely, darling. History is so important. And a founding member? That's impressive, isn't it, John?" My mother gives my father a nudge.

"I didn't know you were interested in history." My father lifts his napkin from his lap and wipes his mouth. His hands are rough from the work he's been doing on the farm, but they're always clean when he's at the table.

"It might have something to do with the other members of the Historical Society." The way Hope says "Historical Society" makes it sound downright criminal. Dirty even.

"Are there many other members?" My mother's perfect pink lips close around her fork, taking a bite of her lunch. She chews contemplatively as she waits for my answer. Sunday lunch is about as formal as we get at the Baker house, so she's dressed in one of her summer sundresses. Rose Baker loves Sunday lunch—putting out the good china and silver, planning the menu, welcoming all her daughters back home—but she does not like gossip and has no idea she's getting ready to contribute to its spread.

"Yes, *Faith*, tell us about the other members." Connie pops a strawberry into her mouth, trying to look innocent.

"Right now there are only three of us: Molly Eagan, myself, and...Cade Allen."

"Cade Allen?" Charity gives me a disappointed look. "I thought this was going to be something juicy. Faith and one of the Allen boys are doing nerdy stuff together? What's interesting about that?"

"History is exceptionally interesting," my mother admonishes. "There is plenty to be learned from history."

Hope waves my mother's comment away. "While history might be interesting, Mama, what's really interesting about this story is how Cade and Faith showed up together and then left together. In the same car. With Cade in the same clothes from the night before." She looks at Connie and they both nod. I can almost see them shivering with delight at having caught me in something even slightly scandalous.

"Cade Allen?" My mother's confused face turns toward me. "Not Charlie?" She seems to have missed the clues my sisters have planted that point to debauchery.

"Charlie isn't in the Historical Society, Mama. Cade's worked with similar businesses and he's being nice enough to help out. We're trying to save the old mill." I shoot a sour look at Hope.

"But he did drive you home from the bachelorette party." Connie isn't going to let this go. "And rumor has it he stayed the night."

"Connie!" My face heats. Even though nothing happened, I'm mortified at the thought of telling the whole embarrassing story to my family. *Little sister can't hold her liquor and needed a babysitter* is a far cry from the sexy situations my sisters would have orchestrated. Any of my sisters in close physical proximity to a man they've been obsessed with for years would have a very different ending than the one I ended up with on Friday. I'm not completely innocent, but compared to the rest of the Baker girls, I am downright virginal.

"Girls!" My father's fist comes down on the tabletop, shaking our glasses of iced tea and rattling the silverware.

We all freeze. "Faith's a grown woman. What she does in the privacy of her house and who she does it with is none of our collective business." He glares at us all. "Now finish eating. Faith and I have to get back to work."

"You shouldn't let your sisters get to you like that." It's said from behind a row of tomatoes so at least I don't have to make eye contact.

"I know, Daddy."

"If you let them keep treating you like a baby..."

"I know." I focus on the weeds in front of me, grateful to have busy hands. Unfortunately, repetitive farm work doesn't engage the brain, and all I've been thinking about are the snappy comebacks I should have had at the ready for my sisters' annoying personal questions. I'm well past the age where my sisters should be able to get my goat that way, but I turn into a ten-year-old when they start in on me.

"Faith, you are a smart and responsible woman. You're the only one of my daughters who's capable of running this business. You have a good head on your shoulders and a kind heart. I don't love hearing about how Cade might or might not have slept over—"

"But he didn't—" I try to interrupt, but my father stops me.

"It doesn't matter if he did or didn't. You're allowed to have a life outside of this farm. Your sisters do and you should too." His voice is soft, and I know he's serious. John Baker doesn't have much use for words, so when he tells me something, I consider myself well and truly told.

"None of them are living happily ever after right now either." It's ugly and I know it. I should be wishing happiness on my sisters. They're all still looking to settle down and have families the same as me. I should send up some good energy instead of the black one I'm feeling right now.

"That's true." My father's eyes sparkle as he looks down at me. "But let's not get petty, now." And then he gives me a wink.

## 11

*Cade*

"Are you sure you have time for this today?"

"Are you sure *you* do? This seems like prime vegetable time right here." I fight the smile my face keeps wanting to give her. I've gone for years being able to battle the attraction I feel for Faith but now it's like the floodgates are suddenly open and I can't hold back the deluge.

"My dad can handle it for a bit. This is important." Faith gives me a solemn nod. "But you have a wedding in a few days and a grand opening... You're maybe too busy to stomp around this run-down mill with me today."

"All those other things are under control." At least, I hope they are. I've done my part, which isn't nearly as hands-on as what is expected of my brothers. I'm the spreadsheet guy, the money man, the abstract problem solver. I'm hardly boots on the ground. Mucking around what used to be the town mill is more of an adventure than I'm usually allowed.

"If you say so." Faith doesn't seem convinced. Undoubtedly Charlie's been talking her ear off about all the things he needs to do. Some of that's real, I'm sure, but some of that's excuses. He's been less and less invested in spending time with Faith and his interest in our new chef has something to do with it.

"Let's check it out then." I motion for Faith to lead the way, and she marches off in front of me. I'm not sure what we're going to find out here. If the parking lot's any indication, Cutter's Mill isn't going to be much to look at. We leave our cars in the tiny dirt patch and try to find the walkway to the buildings. Clumps of grass and weeds poke up from every direction.

"This is pretty overgrown." Faith picks her way along the weedy path. Here's where I give her additional points for not being in the summer outfit Molly would have chosen. Molly may look like something out of *Garden & Gun* with her monogrammed outfits and matching children, but she'd be having trouble today. Faith, on the other hand, is wearing her usual overalls and her feet are protected by a pair of work boots. As she walks along in front of me, I think about offering to trade places. I should really go first and break trail, but I don't want to give up my view of Faith's ass. Everyone else might not find a pair of faded denim overalls to be the sexiest thing a woman can wear, but I've been conditioned to appreciate them. Faith is small, but muscular. She's wearing short sleeves today, and I can see the way her arms have been molded from hours of farm work. I'm not out of shape by any means, but my muscles are more for show. Faith's are for work, for feeding people and paying the bills. Her daily schedule makes my trail runs look like sissy stuff.

"Is that it?" I peer over Faith's shiny blonde head, and there's definitely something in the distance. I can see the outline of red brick, although it lists to the side.

"I hear water so we must be getting close." Faith moves some of the tall grass away from her with her hand. "This could really use ten minutes with a weed wacker. We're going to have to do tick checks when we get out of here."

It has obviously been a while since I've been with a woman if the idea of tick checks has me getting hot and bothered, but that's exactly what happens. I imagine running my hands up and down Faith's arms and legs, and I'm grateful to be walking behind her. As long as she stays facing front, I won't have to explain the situation happening in my pants. *Ticks can get in some pretty tricky spots and I'd have to—*

"Does that qualify as a stream?" Faith looks at me over her shoulder.

"What's the definition of a stream, do you figure?" If I can get my brain to focus on the facts, I'll be able to control the rest of me. That usually works. It's why I like numbers. There isn't all of the gray. That's all black and white, yes and no. The same way me fantasizing about Faith Baker is a no. It shouldn't be happening, no matter what she's told me after a few drinks.

"Well..." Faith stops and puts her hands on her hips. "The mill used to be water-powered so it would have to be a reasonable size. The stream could have been bigger, I guess. Years ago."

From here we can see the water, and it isn't nearly as fast-moving as I would have assumed. It runs behind a building that's obviously leaning to the right. Nothing's been milled here for a while. Hell, it looks like no one's even been out here all year. Or possibly for years. I move next to Faith and our arms brush. She startles, jumping a little. I put the required space between us and survey the area in front of us. There are a few more buildings, all of them in disrepair. If this is what we're saving, I don't have high hopes.

"It looks...dilapidated." There's dismay in my voice. I don't know how invested Faith was in this project, but this glimpse into the work we'll need to do is overwhelming. There's no way we can take on something like this.

"Dilapidated?" Faith considers this. "I was going to say lovely, actually. It's lovely. Look at the patina on that brick. At the wildflowers growing. This could be really fantastic." Oh Lord, she's not giving up; she's digging in.

I want to warn her, let her know how much work lies ahead if we forge on, but I can't bring myself to say any of that when I get a look at her face. I can already see her dreaming about what Cutter's Mill could be, even if I've got no such imagination.

"Should we try to get inside?" I'm encouraging her and I know it. "If it's safe, that is." There, I've added the safety officer caveat. I won't let anything happen to Faith, even if it means carrying her out of here over my shoulder kicking and screaming. Another image I should try not to conjure up too often if my racing heart gives me any clue.

"Could we? Maybe we can peek in the windows." Faith's excitement is contagious, and we both take off toward the mill faster than we should.

We're not ten steps down the path when Faith loses her footing, falling forward in the kind of slow motion scene that would be at home in any horror movie. I'm right behind her, entirely too close for running but luckily close enough to be able to reach out my right hand and catch her arm. Instead of hitting the ground, Faith ends up pulled tightly against my chest and my side takes most of the impact. I roll on my back, taking her with me, barely breathing as Faith pants against my neck.

"Are you okay?" I breathe onto the top of her head.

"Yes." Her breath tickles my neck. "Are you?"

"I think so." Still, I take my time moving, not ready yet to let go of Faith. She tries to prop a little on her elbows, and I stare at her lips. They're close enough for me to kiss her but far enough away to keep me from being impulsive.

Faith blinks down at me. "Have a nice trip, see you next fall."

"What?"

"Sorry. I've never had a chance to say that one." Faith's chest presses against mine. "So inappropriate."

I let my laughter bubble up and overtake me, my entire body shaking. I use it as an excuse to keep one arm wrapped around her. Eventually Faith laughs too, and I get to enjoy thirty more seconds of pretending it's fine to keep her here like this surrounded by the tall grass and the sound of the water gurgling. And in that instant, I decide, if Faith wants to save this crazy place, then I'll do my best to make that a reality.

## 12

*Faith*

Leave it to me to insert a dad joke into an otherwise serious situation. Cade could have been hurt, and the first thing I did was break out the grade-school humor. That was the second time I'd used his body to break my fall, and once again I'd let my nerves get the better of me. *Have a nice trip, see you next fall? Good Lord, Faith. Are you eight years old?* I'm sure Cade loved having another example of how I'm a barely functioning adult. At least he had laughed. *Yeah, but was he laughing with you or at you, genius?* I try to shut off my inner critic for a second, but that only serves to let my inner pervert take over. Being pressed up against Cade makes me have all sorts of ideas I know I shouldn't. I've spent hours thinking about how the hard planes of his chest felt underneath my palms and—imagine the way my sisters would react!—the way they'd felt rubbing against my breasts as he laughed. I could get used to having Cade's arm around me and his face close enough to see the sandy flecks in the stubble on his chin. He'd been in kissing distance if I'd been a little more daring, if I'd been sure that was what he wanted. He had had this look in his eyes that I couldn't read. Was it amusement? Or was it interest? Now I'll never know because in addition to being the clumsiest woman on the planet around him, I'm also unable to keep my mouth from spewing out nonsense.

"So how was the mill?" My father's voice knocks me back into reality. I'm supposed to be working on the invoices, not daydreaming about Cade Allen's chest. And hands. And mouth. And— "Worth driving over there?"

"It was. You would not believe the way those buildings have aged. They're all at least a hundred years old and they look like something out of a movie, the way things have grown up around them." Cade had frowned at the trees sprouting from the side of the old general store and had made an unhappy grunting sound at the way the old water wheel was hanging off the mill, but he hadn't said he thought it was impossible. "Cade's going to try to get Chance to go over there and take a look to see if he thinks it's structurally sound."

"Did Cade think that might be an issue?" My father's brows knit together. There's more gray in there than blond now, and they could use a trim.

"Maybe. They're old, obviously, and there's a level of disrepair." I don't fill him in on the field mice I'm sure are living in more than just the open meadow. "But it really is beautiful. Full of potential."

"Did Cade agree with that?"

"Eventually." I keep my head down so I don't have to see my father's face.

"You talked him into it?" There's a hint of a laugh there that I try to ignore. "You could sell underwear to a nudist, Faith."

"Tell that to Henry down at Ham & Eggs. I can't get him

to even *try* making anything with the kale I keep putting in their order every week. Like folks in Mint Springs don't deserve to enjoy a kale salad like the rest of the civilized world."

"I'm sure he'll eventually come around. How are the rest of the orders looking?" We've been trying to become one of the premiere farms for supplying local restaurants. So far, we've been doing well convincing places to trust us instead of buying from the big conglomerates. Our margins are razor thin, though, and I'm hoping Charlie and his family's new restaurant will be the account that turns that around.

"Good, I think. We're still not turning a huge profit, but we aren't losing money. The Allens might help us with that once they get up and running, and I think I've got a few other places closer to Atlanta ready to at least give us a try."

"You got the order for the wedding all squared away?"

Normally my daddy would want to take a look at the order, make sure I've calculated everything correctly. I get ready to hand over the paperwork for Cooper and Hadley's wedding. The new chef has stuck to Southern classics, for the most part, although she cleaned me out of *haricot verts*, and I'm interested to see how she uses those next to all the grits and greens. I'll drop the order this afternoon so Jenna can get a head start on the presentation for tomorrow. I hold out the stack of papers in my hand.

"No need. You haven't made a mistake yet. I'd be wasting time checking your work. You're as good at running a business as you are shooting a buck and baiting a hook. Should have known you'd be a quick study." He gives me a sly smile. "Can't have my star employee thinking I don't trust her."

"I'm your only employee, Daddy." But I puff up with pride all the same.

When I'd agreed to work with my father, I'd had some

reservations. As the lone tomboy in a family that could have used a few sons to balance all the estrogen out, there were plenty of things my dad was happy to teach me. I've always felt more at home jumping off a rope swing than sitting on the bank. Never thought twice about choosing softball over cheerleading. He's never made me feel like any of those activities weren't options for me, and I grew up with the skinned knees and filthy play clothes to prove it. But working together was different. He's always said I was smart, but I'm his daughter. Of course he expects to be the boss. Him giving me more responsibility lets me know he isn't taking me for granted.

"Would now be a good time to ask for that raise?" I tilt my head to the side and wait for his reaction.

"Raise? Faith Caroline Baker, have you lost your mind?"

"Doesn't hurt to ask." I learned that from him too.

"No, I suppose it doesn't." The tiny tilt of the side of his mouth tells me he approves of the question even if he's giving me no for an answer. "Maybe try again in a month or two."

*Cade*

"Hey, thanks for helping Faith for me." Charlie makes himself comfortable next to me on the porch step. "I really appreciate it."

"No problem." I'm not about to tell Charlie I'm a million miles away from good deed status. I'm not helping Faith as a favor to him. I'm helping her so I can selfishly spend more time with her. I take another sip of my whiskey.

"What are you doing with Faith?" Chance's question activates all the guilt I'm feeling right now.

"I roped Cade into helping her with the Historical Society stuff." Charlie looks entirely too pleased with himself, like he's tricked me into giving him all my Halloween candy. He actually has done that. I was in first grade and he was in second. This time, though, it's me who's doing the stealing, for once, and I feel less upset about it than I would have expected.

"The thing with the mill?" Chance pours himself a drink from the bottle we've brought out on the porch. "Move over a bit; I'm getting too fat to sit out here." He groans as he settles himself on a wooden step. "I hope I can still fit into my suit tomorrow. Mae really loaded me up with the coconut cake tonight. I still can't believe Cooper's getting married. Two down, two to go." He lifts his tumbler for Charlie and I to clink against, but neither of us raises our glass.

"I'll toast to Cooper and Hadley, but don't go putting me in any kind of marriage mess." I shake my head.

"Oh, come on." Chance keeps his drink in the air. "I know it isn't on either of your radars, but never say never, right?"

Charlie gives in and lets the edge of his glass touch Chance's. "Never say never."

I still refuse to move my drink anywhere but to my lips. "No way. I'm not even tempting the universe by pretending to participate in that." I down the rest of my whiskey in one gulp and reach for the bottle.

"You'd be lucky to find someone who would put up with your serious ass." Chance grumbles.

"And that grumpy attitude," Charlie adds. "It's worse in the morning. Imagine the woman who would put up with that." He and Chance exchange knowing looks.

"She'd be a ballbuster alright. Either that or a pushover. No matter what, she'd be no fun. That's guaranteed." Chance is egging me on, but I'm not about to take the bait.

"Oh, like what's-her-name from high school. Remember her? So serious. Captain of the debate team and probably main organizer for the Purity Ball." Charlie elbows Chance in the side and they both laugh. "What was her name, Cade? Marsha? Or Mary? Something with the letter M."

"Like I'd tell you." I concentrate on my drink. "Don't you have things to do to get ready for tomorrow?"

"I do, but I thought I'd spend a few more minutes here.

Let my dinner settle before I face whatever's going on in the kitchen." Charlie stretches his arms up over his head. "I am glad I'm not the one getting married tomorrow."

"Cooper seems more than fine with it," Chance volunteers and reaches for the bottle. "He seems excited about all of it. Marriage, the baby. I've never seen him happier, honestly."

That's the truth. But why wouldn't our oldest brother be happy? We opened his distillery, and business is looking good. He's making it official with the girl he's loved forever. Even this surprise baby is good news. He and Hadley are excited to be parents, and they still have the luxury of thinking love can last forever.

I, however, am not so lucky.

"Who's in charge of Mom tomorrow? It has to be one of you since I'll be running the restaurant and Cooper'll be getting hitched." Charlie acts like there's even a question who'll be given that assignment.

"That's gotta be Cade. He's her favorite." Chance pretends he's teasing, but I know he thinks it's true. My brothers all think our mother favors me. I'm the baby, and they all complain I've been coddled within an inch of my life. In truth, I have the closest relationship with my mother because I was the only one still at home when our father finally moved out for good.

"I'm not her favorite," I protest, but it won't do any good. It won't change the way she'll automatically reach for my arm if I'm standing near her or the way she'll assume I'm going to be the one to make sure she has what she needs.

"I guess it's good Dad decided not to come." It's hard to miss the bitterness in Chance's voice. "But what can you expect?" Our father was busy on Chance's wedding day too.

He couldn't be bothered to drive down from Nashville to see the first of his children say *I do*.

"At least they won't be fighting." Charlie shrugs. "Little blessings."

I keep my thoughts on that to myself. My brothers think they know what they're talking about when it comes to our parents and the end of their marriage, but they don't know the half of it. Only I was there to witness the worst of it, to hear the awful things they said to one another.

"I'll drink to that." Chance clinks his glass with Charlie's.

Once again, I keep my drink to myself. "I'm going to see if Sadie and Mae need any help inside."

My brothers let me slip away without protest. They don't need a killjoy keeping them from enjoying their drinks, and I don't need to spend any more time poking at the hurt that always follows me when I think of our parents' divorce.

It is the rainiest day of the year, possibly the rainiest day of all time. If Noah floated by on his ark full of animals, I would not be surprised. This rain is threatening to ruin Cooper and Hadley's wedding, and we're all scrambling to try and save what we can of their perfect outdoor ceremony. It turns out that really only means moving the flowers inside the distillery. The only saving grace here is that the distillery building holds a special place in Hadley and Cooper's hearts. Otherwise, I imagine we'd have a bride throwing herself on the floor in despair instead of the one who eventually comes floating up the aisle.

But before that happens, I get to witness Faith Baker do the same thing. I know the spotlight should be on Hadley—and she looks beautiful—but Faith catches me by surprise again. With all the weather issues, the first time I see her all day is when she starts her way down the aisle. I'm standing with my brothers, staring straight ahead and trying to remember not to lock my knees. I've made that mistake before, and the rest of third grade was all about how I fainted during the Christmas pageant. Which, as I think about it, wasn't the worst thing a third grader could have done during an hour-long program of nothing but boring holiday music. I'm trying to do that slight bend—the kind that doesn't call attention—and attempting to time it to every minute or so, but I forget completely about my knees or the possibility of fainting once Faith appears at the end of the makeshift aisle we've constructed.

Her hair's down again, wavy around her face, and I swear Hadley's chosen a shade of blue for the bridesmaid dresses that exactly matches Faith's eyes. And those eyes are looking straight at me as she takes those excruciatingly slow steps toward the front of the distillery. There's no reason for me not to look my fill as she walks—we're supposed to be looking at the girls. There isn't a good excuse, however, for the ridiculous smile that overtakes my face when her eyes lock with mine. There's even less of a reason for Faith's smile to answer mine and her gaze to stay on my face all the way down the aisle. I've never really understood when folks talk about being the only people in the room or having time stop. That's all been bullshit for me.

Until now.

Charlie's next to me, and when he realizes who Faith's looking at, he makes sure to pull me out of my fantasy. That's all it is, really. Faith Baker's confessed her feelings, and they're ones I can't really return for multiple reasons. Still, it's nice to imagine pairing off with her after the ceremony the way Chance and Cooper will with their wives. I picture dancing with her when the band starts and holding her hand under the table as Chance gives what's sure to be a sappy speech at dinner. She'd give my hand a squeeze and look at me when he got ridiculous, like we had some kind of inside joke.

But Charlie's frown washes all of that away. This isn't a fantasy. And Faith isn't going to be mine. Not now and not ever.

## 14

*Faith*

I tingle all over for the entire ceremony. Thank goodness we aren't in a church because I'm sure the Lord would have struck me dead for all the sinful thoughts that flood my mind when Cade locks eyes with me. I should also give thanks for Hadley's sense of style, because the dresses she chose for us to wear are nothing short of miraculous. For a girl who doesn't love wearing much other than overalls, I am feeling exceptionally princess-y today. We've had hair and make up done in the way only Hadley could have arranged. Leave it to a woman who does hair for a living to convince the entire staff of her family's salon to come in to take care of her family and bridal party. The Crawford women alone needed five stylists.

Hadley's grandmother is wearing the shiniest outfit I've ever seen, and her mother isn't exactly holding the sparkle, but neither of them outshines the bride. Pregnant or not, Hadley is radiant. It might be raining outside, but nothing was going to dampen her spirits. She was sipping on some lemonade Jenna'd sent up from the restaurant while the rest of us helped ourselves to champagne.

"You ready?" Lily fluffed out the back of Hadley's white dress. It's simple, but elegant, with a loose waistline that makes her bump an asset and not a detractor.

"I've *been* ready." Hadley's eyes sparkled as we got loaded up to try to get to the distillery without getting covered in mud. We picked our way across the little rivers that had formed in Hadley and Cooper's driveway, careful not to get any wetter than we had to.

And we had arrived right as a giant rainbow flung itself across the Georgia sky. There were more than a few gasps over that little miracle. But that rainbow's got nothing on the look Cade Allen was giving me as I walked toward him up the aisle. I wasn't really walking toward him, of course. He just happened to be conveniently on my way to the altar the boys had somehow thrown together once the ceremony got moved indoors. Those eyes boring into me, seeming to like what they saw, still has me buzzing once photos are done and we're mingling for the cocktail hour.

"Make sure you don't overdo it." Charlie's voice comes from close to my ear and I jump, spilling a bit of my gin fizz.

"Goodness, Charlie." I try to shake the drops of my cocktail from my wet hand.

"Sorry. You seemed deep in thought over here." He leans against the side of the table.

"Zoning out, really." I don't dare tell Charlie I was trying to hold on to the feeling of his brother's eyes on me for as long as possible.

"You look pretty. Haven't seen you in a dress in a while." It's a compliment, but coming from Charlie it doesn't mean as much as it might from another man. He's always been quicker to compliment my abilities than my appearance, and until recently I've always appreciated that. Lately, though, I'd love to have someone interested in my looks, as shallow as that might seem.

"Hadley was generous. She could have been a real bridezilla, but we all look great, I think." I find Hadley and Cooper across the room. He's looking at her like she's the most amazing thing he's ever seen, and I get a tiny little pang of jealousy deep in my chest. I try to push it down and replace it with happiness. Hadley and Cooper have managed to find each other despite obstacles; that should be a good sign for me, something that gives me hope.

I manage to keep that hopeful smile on my face as I look around the room. Now that the pressure of the ceremony's gone, everyone is starting to loosen up, and I'm thinking about a second drink.

"How are things going with your thing?" Charlie's trying to make conversation, but his attention's obviously elsewhere.

"My thing?"

"The thing with Cade."

The tingling returns, and I try to act like my stomach isn't filling with butterflies. "You mean the mill?"

"Sure." His eyes scan the room.

"It's fine, we haven't had to do much yet. We went to look at the building—"

"Do you think we have enough food up here?" Charlie looks around again. "How many things have you tasted?"

"A few. The grits cake. Some other pastry thing." I follow Charlie's eyes to the door. "Are you waiting for someone?"

"Jenna should be up here by now. Maybe I should go down to the restaurant and see what's keeping her." He downs the rest of his drink. "I'll catch up with you later." And he walks away before I can say anything else. So much for my attentive best friend. He was barely listening to a word I said.

"See you later," I mumble under my breath and make my way to the bar. It is definitely time for a refill.

"You look really beautiful, Faith." There's the compliment I've been waiting for. Cade's words snake up my spine. They're more intoxicating than any alcohol, more potent than any drug could ever be. I turn around slowly and tilt my face up. If we were more than friends, he'd lean down and press his lips to mine, maybe slide a hand through my hair. He doesn't do this, of course, because we're barely anything at all to each other, not to mention the fact that we're standing in the middle of his oldest brother's wedding reception.

"Thank you. You look nice too. Very handsome." He's more than handsome, but it isn't the time or the place to tell him any of that. There will never be a time or place for that. I've got plenty of colorful adjectives to describe Cade in his suit, broad shoulders blocking me from seeing anything or anyone else. The butterflies in my belly take flight.

He ducks his head a fraction. Is he shy? Unsure? "Can I get you a drink?"

I let him order another gin fizz for me, his hands resting on the edge of the bar as we wait. "Charlie gave me a little lecture about not drinking too much. He doesn't want a repeat of the other night, I guess."

Cade turns toward me, the full force of those hazel eyes nearly knocking me over. "I wouldn't mind a repeat of that. Not at all." His cheeks flush a bit. "Save a dance for me, okay?" He hands me my drink and walks away.

What in the heck?

## 15

*Cade*

*Idiot.*

What had I been thinking? I hadn't been. Not really. I'd let myself pretend I was someone I'm not for a second, and that was a second too long. What was I expecting Faith to say when I told her I'd be happy with a repeat of the other night? *Sure, I'd like to get blackout drunk again and not remember a damn thing, Cade. Sounds fun.* I'd been talking about the kiss, but Faith doesn't know that. So I'd sounded like a fool. Luckily, I'd had the good sense to walk away. I'd still danced with Faith once the band started up, but I hadn't asked for another, and I'd tried my best to keep my distance for the rest of the night. It was torture, but I'd done it.

That doesn't explain why in the world I'm sitting at the bar this morning waiting for Faith to deliver the restaurant's vegetable order. I got up early to hit the trails, but never quite made it. Stopping in the one place I knew there'd be fresh coffee and ending up looking at last week's expenses just sort of happened. In the back of my mind, I'm justifying this choice with my favorite new excuse— the Mint Springs

Historical Society. I might have never given old buildings a second thought until a few weeks ago, but now I'm all in. We need to talk about next steps for the mill. But pretending to be in the right place at the right time is a roundabout way of seeing her twice. I could set up a meeting easier if I sent her a text, but that would also mean texting Molly. And would eliminate the possibility of seeing Faith's smiling face today, which I was up all night thinking about.

I know all of these choices are setting me up for a fall. Faith's drunken confession might have given me an excuse, but I still know there can't be anything between us. That might have been my excuse for why I never made a move before, when I was terrified of having Faith shoot me down, but even now all the things she deserves that I can't possibly give her bounce around in my head like a pinball. The punch in the face Charlie'd give me is small potatoes to the possibility of eventually breaking her heart. And I know I would, because despite what my brothers might think with their dreamy weddings and heartfelt forevers, I've seen what all that's really like in the end. I won't do that to anyone and would die before I'd risk hurting Faith.

"You're here early." Charlie's extremely chipper this morning.

"I was going for a run, but I got sidetracked." There, early morning lie completely set up.

"You don't have to keep going over the expenses. I know what I'm doing." Charlie's a little indignant, and normally I would try to smooth that over. Working together is tough enough without their being hard feelings over nothing. But if I tell him I'm here wasting time, not only will he know my real motives, he'll also try to put a stop to them.

"I like to look periodically. That's all." I choose some arbitrary expense. "Linens were a lot this week."

"Because we just finished up an event, dumb ass. Maybe you remember it? Cooper got married. It was kind of a big deal." Charlie's smile is officially a scowl. "Wait, I know you remember it because you spent all night staring at Faith. Care to explain that?"

I most certainly do not, and having her come walking in the front door hauling a giant box of vegetables is not the saving grace I would have imagined. My face betrays me, lighting up in a way I know Charlie can't miss. "Can I help you with that?" I use chivalry as an excuse to put a little space between Charlie and my grinning face. Faith gives me the crate willingly. It's heavier than it looks, and I wonder how she's been able to make it look so easy to carry.

"Wasn't expecting to see you here." Faith wipes her hands on the front of her overalls.

"Cade's here micromanaging things," Charlie mutters. He comes up next to Faith and stays there, making us an awkward triangle.

Faith's eyes can't seem to find a good place to land. "Mind if I help myself to coffee?"

"Like you need to ask. Like you *ever* ask." Charlie calls after her. She's already behind the bar reaching for a mug. "Don't you have someone else to bother?" Already Charlie's had enough of me, but I'm not here to see him, so I don't run off like I might have in the past.

"I actually need to talk to Faith now that she's here."

"Yeah? That's lucky then, that you were here when she showed up." Charlie's raised eyebrow is an accusation.

"Exceptionally lucky." I nod. "Saves me a text."

"A text about what?" Faith looks at me over the rim of her coffee cup, and I momentarily forget what I was talking about. It doesn't help that most of this is an elaborate ruse to get to spend time with her. I'm not great at deception, and it shows.

"Apparently, Cade here was going to text you, but now that you're here he can talk to you in person." Charlie cocks his head to the side and gives me the kind of grin he used to when he thought he was about to watch me crash and burn. I've done it enough times for it to be predictable now, but this time I'm not trying to jump my bike from one side of the river to the other or attempting to convince one of the local girls to let me kiss her behind Bootlegger. My reason to see Faith is one hundred percent on the up and up, even if my reasons for pursuing it might not be.

"About the Historical Society. I did some research about nonprofit structure and thought you and Molly might want to get together to talk about it. Chance is going by the mill today, so we'll see what he thinks about that. Maybe we should schedule something? For tomorrow?" I try to make it sound like a business meeting and not a date. Molly would be with us, and, anyway, wasn't it Charlie's idea to have me help out? He can't be mad about me doing what he wanted.

But he is. Not enough for me to give up, but enough to have me taking a step back when Faith throws her arms around me. Coffee sloshes out of her cup and onto the floor, and Charlie's mouth fixes itself into a hard, thin line.

"Oh my gosh! You are the best, Cade. Charlie, you were right. Cade's the perfect person to help out with this." Faith's eyes shine, and she bounces a little on the toes of her boots. "I'll call Molly on my way back to Happy Trails." She does one of her excited shivers and claps her hands together before she goes running out the door.

I'm still trying to deal with the impromptu hug from Faith when Charlie turns on me. "Watch yourself, little brother."

"What does that mean?"

"Faith gets attached, and I don't want you pulling one of your disappearing acts on her. If you tell her you're going to do something, you damn well better do it." Charlie means business.

"Disappearing act? I don't do that." *Do I?* I take a gulp of my coffee.

"You do. But you'd better not do it to Faith if she needs you for this historical thing, whatever the hell that is." He throws a hand in the air.

I'm the most dependable of all my brothers, no contest. The only one who always does what he says. Whatever Charlie's talking about isn't something I'm worried about because it isn't true.

## 16

*Faith*

"I'm going to officially call this meeting of the Mint Springs Historical Society to order."

I try not to make eye contact with Cade, fairly certain his face has the same surprised look as mine. Molly has gone all out for this meeting—fancy snacks and color-coded file folders. That's not the part that has me suppressing a chuckle, though. It's the gavel Molly seems determined to use. For a group with only three members, it seems a little much.

"First order of business, roll call." Molly's standing at the head of her dining room table, once again dressed in a crisp summer dress, her monogram embroidered on her chest. She's been nice enough to invite us into her home for this meeting. Unfortunately, she's taking the idea very seriously.

"I don't think we need to—"

Molly silences Cade with a menacing wave of her gavel. "Say 'present' when I call your name." She pauses. Is she looking at a list of our names? "Cade Allen."

"Um, present?" Cade's wide eyes meet mine across the space of the dark wood table.

"Excellent." I swear Molly puts a check by his name. "Faith Baker."

I blink a few times. She cannot be serious. "I'm here."

"You're *present*." Another check on the paper in front of Molly. "Now we can get started." She reorganizes the stack of papers in front of her.

"I thought we could talk a little about the struct—"

"Ah, ah. Wait a second, Cade. Before we introduce any new business, we need to go over the *old* business." Molly clears her throat. "What I'd really love is if this meeting you could take the minutes, Faith."

"The minutes?" Why do I feel like I'm trapped in middle school all of a sudden, and I've been made secretary of the student council?

"Jot down some notes, so we'll remember what we talked about. We don't have any from last meeting, and that's going to make us a little sparse on the old business." Molly slides a legal pad and a freshly sharpened pencil toward me. "You don't mind, do you?"

I do, but I'm surprised enough not to fight her. Molly runs her own business, but it's a one-woman show. I doubt she's spent much time bossing people around other than her children. Not lately, at least. I can imagine her terrorizing her Girl Scout troop in elementary school or some church choir as a teenager. Molly seems more than ready to flex those leadership muscles here with me and Cade.

"I thought we were doing things a little more informally." Cade's comment does nothing to stop Molly's steamrolling.

"But is informal really the best way for us to start out in

this organization?" Molly's already telegraphing the answer with a sad shake of her head.

"No?" Cade's answer probably isn't supposed to sound like a question. I wonder if that's the kind of thing I should "jot down."

"No," Molly confirms, and Cade's eyebrows nearly hit the ceiling. "Eventually we'll have more members and we need to start off on the right foot. Start the way you intend to finish, right?"

I'm not sure I'll want to finish anything that starts with Molly lording that gavel over me, but I dutifully write down "start and finish." It's gibberish, but it still counts as jotting, in my opinion. I steal another glance at Cade's shocked face. I'm sure he's regretting his decision to help me right about now. His brow stays furrowed as Molly commandeers the meeting for twenty more excruciating minutes as she lays out her plans for how the Historical Society meetings should be run. By the time she gets to new business, I'm sure Cade's ready to bolt out of Molly's McMansion and run screaming down the street.

By the time we finally get to talking about the mill, I'm ready for a nap. Cade's explanation of how we should set up the business side of things wasn't particularly riveting, but it gave me a chance to unabashedly stare at him. He was saying things about donations and foundations, but I was concentrating on the dimple in his chin. Do all the Allens have one? Twice he takes a second to sip his coffee and needs to get a drop or two from his top lip with his tongue. I nearly faint.

"That's a great idea, don't you think, Faith?"

"Huh?" Not only am I terrible at taking notes, I'm not even great at pretending to pay attention.

"The foundation idea. So we can get started on raising

money for the mill." Molly's disapproving eyes focus on mine.

"Oh, yes. Let me put that down here..." I make a show of scribbling something on the note pad, and I swear I hear Cade stifle a laugh.

"Which brings me to the next item I have on my agenda for new business." Molly's giant smile and sly look should clue me in. She's obviously got something big planned—the kind of thing I don't have time for and neither does Cade—but we both wait for her grand announcement like a pair of sitting ducks. When Molly claps her hands together, the glee is palpable. "A fair!"

"Excuse me?" Cade leans forward.

"A country fair. Or a harvest festival. Or whatever. An event to get the community involved." Molly's pleased enough with herself to finally sit down.

"Where would we be having this event, exactly?" I can't be the only one with questions.

"At the mill, of course. It would be a chance to get donors for the project and for us to establish the place as a community hub, like it used to be. It's a great idea, don't you think?" Molly leans back in her chair. "Did y'all get a chance to try the lemonade?" She gestures to the pitcher in the center of the table.

"Forget about the lemonade. We can't pull off an event at the mill, Molly. We don't own it and we're not even sure the current owners would be willing to sell it." Cade gives me an exasperated look.

"He's right, Molly. If we want to use the event to solicit donations to buy the place, how are we going to pull that off? Aside from the fact that we'd need permission, it isn't exactly safe." Chance had said he thought the buildings were salvageable, but they aren't in great shape. "What kind of a timeline are we talking about here?"

Molly's bottom lip comes out in an exaggerated pout. "Well, I'd been thinking it could happen in the fall. Think about how pretty it'd be with the leaves turning. It'd be a big draw for sure as long as we worked around the high school football schedule."

"There are a lot of things we'd need to get done before we could even think about anything like that." Cade starts counting on his fingers. "There's the permits and the permission to actually use the place, not to mention the work to get it up to any kind of code. We'd need to set up our foundation and try to get a few more members. We can't possibly do all of the work just the three of us. We've all got other obligations. And this isn't Vermont; North Georgia isn't exactly famous for its foliage." Already he's out of fingers and we haven't even gotten started.

"But you've seen the place." Molly turns those big eyes on me. "You said yourself it's lovely. Think of how great it would be to have a farmer's market there once a week. Or as an additional place to showcase local businesses. If we had events there with sponsorships..." Molly's been thinking long term and the market idea does get my attention. Plus, I did fall in love with those old buildings.

I look across the table at Cade. He's gotten roped into something much bigger than he planned, that much is for sure. He looks from Molly to me like we've escaped from the insane asylum.

"We can at least try, can't we?" Molly's plea is designed to get us to agree one tiny step at a time. Cade and I both know it will be more than trying if we agree to her plan. But it's still hard to say no, especially if it means more time with

Cade as we try to figure out how to take the mill from trash to treasure.

Our silence apparently means acceptance, because a huge grin takes over Molly's face. "Cookie?" she offers, pushing the plate full of homemade chocolate chip cookies into the center of the table. Cade and I both take one and seal our fate.

## 17

*Cade*

*How did I get myself in this mess? I don't give even one good goddamn about history or an old mill! I should step away from all of this before I get tangled up any further. That would be the best thing to do, because there's nothing tying me to this project or the Historical Society.*

Except Faith.

Watching her during that nightmare of a meeting had made it almost bearable. Molly was really on a roll, and Faith's got no poker face. Every new surprise showed like a movie in high definition. It was almost worth it to be able to see her brow wrinkle up and her mouth drop open every time Molly made a new pronouncement.

"What's got you smiling over here?" Debbie's probably been watching me for two full minutes.

"Nothing." I'm not known for smiling and certainly not for grinning like crazy while sitting alone at the counter at Ham & Eggs. Debbie's most likely about to call one of my brothers to come and pick me up on account of me being daytime drunk. "How are you, Debbie?" Anywhere else I could go ahead and order my sandwich and be done with it, but here in Mint Springs you have to get the pleasantries out first.

"I'm fine. You eating alone?" She licks the point of her pencil even though she knows my order by heart. There won't be any need to write it down.

"I'm actually going to get it to go. I need to get back to work." My time at Molly's, as amusing as it might have been, means I'm behind on things at home. Already the mill is taking up too much time.

"Suit yourself. You want the usual?"

"Yes, ma'am. Turkey on whole grain. Side of fries." I hand her the menu I never bother reading. "Please."

"I'll have it out in a few. You want a Coke while you wait? Tea?" Debbie asks even though she knows I'm going to tell her the same thing I always do.

"Water's fine, thanks."

I've barely had two sips when Faith comes barreling through the restaurant door. She scans the room until her eyes settle on me, then she makes a beeline to where I'm sitting at the counter. Determined Faith is always like a tornado, and this time it's coming straight for me.

"I thought I might find you here." She's out of breath and her cheeks are flushed.

"Did you run here?" I'm not entirely joking. "Sit. Take a break." I make sure to give her plenty of space as I try to convince her to take the stool next to mine.

"I can't stay. All that crazy at Molly's has me runnin' behind." Faith is working hard at catching her breath.

"It was crazy, right? It wasn't just me?" I let a little of the surprise I felt at Molly's tactics show on my face.

"With a capital C. Somebody must have recently found an old copy of *Robert's Rules of Order*. It felt like being held hostage by a deranged Betty Crocker." Faith rolls her eyes. "That's why I came looking for you. You didn't sign up for any of that, and I don't want you to feel obligated to help out. Molly's idea of how things should be is over the top. I wanted you to know you can back out and there'll be no hard feelings." She finally takes a deep breath. "There. I said it. Save yourself while you have the opportunity."

I let the laugh I've been holding in come tumbling out. "It's a little too late for that."

Faith's brow furrows, and I want to take my thumb and smooth out that wrinkle. "Too late?"

"I think we're in too deep to ever get free of Molly Eagan." That part's probably true. Disappointing Molly would have long-term effects.

"Be serious. You've got a pretty full plate." Faith finally sits down, her knees dangerously close to mine.

"You're plate's full too. I know running that farm and managing deliveries takes up a good amount of time. Don't pretend you've been sitting at home eating bonbons. Making a business successful isn't easy." Faith's up before the sun and hits the ground running. Before my first cup of coffee, she's already put in a full day. "But you're making time for this."

"That doesn't mean *you* have to. Why would you?"

I can't exactly confess my real reason for staying involved. The chance to spend time with Faith has basically fallen into my lap. I'd be a fool not to take advantage of it, but I'd also be a fool to let it affect the commitments I already have. "It's important to you."

Faith blinks. "So?"

"So... I promised Charlie I'd help you." I chicken out. Of course I do. I'm not supposed to be interested in Faith, and I'm not supposed to know she might see me as more than a friend, but I can't help wanting to be close to that. "You need a numbers guy, someone who isn't attached to the project in the way you and Molly are." I leave out my own already dangerous *attachment*.

"I'm not attached." Faith's mouth works itself into an indignant almost pout.

"I saw the way you looked at that building. No one talks about moss or uses the word patina if they're being strictly analytical." I take a sip of my water. "Do you want lunch?" I look for Debbie, but for once she isn't hovering.

"And you can be strictly analytical?" It's said like a challenge, and I already know I can't be. About the physical building? Sure. About the way I'm starting to let myself feel when I'm close to Faith? Absolutely not.

"You will never hear me wax poetic about the light or the wildflowers or the sound of the stream, that's for sure. But I will let you know if there's no way we can make our budget work or if you and Molly need to scale back those grand plans of yours." That's why I'm the best person to be the CFO for my family's business. I love the farm, but I'm not attached to the restaurant or the distillery the way my brothers are. I didn't fall in love in my grandfather's farmhouse and decide I couldn't possibly live anywhere else. I'm playing with fire a little bit here with Faith, but playing's all I'm doing. I know better than to do more than dip my toe in when it comes to the way she makes my chest ache.

"I can be analytical too," Faith protests as she takes the sweet tea Debbie brings over without even having to ask if that's what Faith might want.

Debbie snorts. "Faith Baker, if anyone's governed by their heart, it's you. No one in here believes you can leave emotion out of a darn thing."

"Sure I can. I'm not even sure I want to work on saving

the mill. How do you like that?" Faith cocks her head to the side with more than a hint of defiance.

"Then why are we even bothering to talk about it?" The bell from the kitchen dings, and Henry slides my sandwich in the window. "Glad we figured that out before I had to leave."

Faith bites her bottom lip, her teeth leaving the slightest indentation in the juicy red of her mouth. "But it would be nice to be able to have a permanent place for a farmer's market..."

"See? You're already thinking about it. Emotionally." I hand Debbie a twenty and wave away the change.

"That's a *business* decision, Cade." Faith nods, agreeing with herself. "All business."

"If it was all business, you'd be thinking about existing places to have a farmers market, not dreaming about a new place that requires all your sweat equity." I sneak a fry from the brown paper bag in front of me and tilt the bag toward Faith. Her hand snakes inside.

"But that's how I always do it. I think about the future and how perfect it could be." She chews.

"And I think of the money it takes. The man hours."

"That's why we'd be a good team." Faith is hesitant, but her face is hopeful. Those mesmerizing eyes look up at me, and I lose all sense. She's got a super power, and she doesn't even know it.

"I tell you what, if you want to try to make this happen, I'm still in to help. But we do it our way, not Molly's. She can't be running this show." The panic I feel at giving in to an idea that's getting crazier and crazier by the minute is easily squashed by the way my heart nearly stops when Faith smiles.

"You sure?"

"Not at all, but let's see what we can do. Order something and we'll talk about it." I motion for Debbie, who's already on her way over with a plate for my lunch. What's another hour away from the farm?

"I take it the Historical Society's back on?" Debbie's raised eyebrow over the back of Faith's head is only for me.

"For now." Faith's words may seem cautious, but she's bouncing a little in her seat. "Can we still think about a fall festival?"

What was I saying before? Oh yeah, how did I get myself in this mess? I think the answer's sitting right next to me.

## 18

*Faith*

"Molly did not take that well." I announce it as I walk in the door to Cade's office, before I have the good sense to make sure he's alone. He isn't. Jenna's sitting in one of the leather chairs across from his desk, and she does not look happy. Or maybe that's just her everyday face. I send up a tiny prayer of contrition for being so rude. It isn't like me to dislike someone as fiercely as I do Jenna, but it isn't every day that my best friend starts to go loco over some woman, especially one so prickly.

Cade looks up from the papers on his desk and gives me the kind of smile that warms more than my heart. I am definitely not complaining about his welcome. Jenna's scowl I can do without, but Cade's happy face just for me? That almost makes up for it.

"Sorry to interrupt," I apologize and try to give Jenna an exceptionally contrite face. Not that she'd notice. But I barged in on what looks like a meeting for Cade's real business with some information about our fake one, so I need to remember my place. Although fake isn't the right word.

Pretend? No. Either way, the mill and the Historical Society are low on the totem pole when it comes to Cade's time.

"We were finishing." Cade stands, and I can see how much taller he is than Jenna. She's wearing flats instead of her usual super high heels, and Cade towers over her. All of the Allens are tall, with booming voices and broad shoulders that can be intimidating.

Jenna doesn't seem the least bit scared, though. She squares her shoulders and barely gives me a nod on her way out the door. She throws a, "Thanks, Cade. Let me know what else you need," over her shoulder, and she's gone. The only thing left to prove she was here at all is the lingering scent of her spicy perfume and the plate of what looks like pastry on Cade's desk.

"What was she worked up about?" I'm almost afraid to ask. Jenna has a temper, and I don't know if I really want to hear the latest story.

"She wasn't worked up." Cade's eyebrows knit together. "What made you think that?"

"Jenna always seems a little annoyed." I shrug like it's no big deal and not something that makes me slightly furious.

"That's her way, I think. She gets right to the point. Doesn't waste time with the pleasantries, if you know what I mean. She doesn't mean anything by it. Do you want to sit?" He gestures to the club chairs, and I choose the one that is not currently still warm from Jenna Bard's butt.

I expect Cade to sit back down at his desk but he comes around to Jenna's chair and sits down there. "*Empanada*?"

"I'm not sure I know what that is." I look down at the plate of flaky pastry Cade's holding out.

"They're savory, I think. Jenna makes them." He gives the plate another push toward me. "Try one."

I take one and inspect it before I bite into it. I don't want to seem rude again, but I also don't want to be poisoned. Although, Jenna meant these for Cade so they're probably safe. I chew, letting the flavors hit my tongue.

They're delicious. Tiny pastry pockets of seasoned meat. Beef, I think. And potatoes I'm pretty sure I grew myself. I must begrudgingly admit again that Jenna is all that and a can of cheese when it comes to this chef stuff. It's unfair to have her kind of confidence, exude sex appeal, and be able to bring a man to his knees with your cooking too. What have I got to compare with that? Cade might not be interested in Jenna, but he isn't going to be wooed by my turnips, no matter how gorgeous they are.

"You said Molly had an issue with our proposal? I knew I should have helped you talk to her." Cade takes a bite of his empanada and closes his eyes. I try to keep from rolling mine.

"She does not like relinquishing the throne." That's the understatement of the year. Molly had all but stomped her feet and pitched a fit like one of her children when I'd told her Cade and I wanted to reorganize things a bit.

"We don't need a queen; we need worker bees. She understands that, right?" Another bite, another near groan from Cade over Jenna's cooking. "These are sooo good." The sounds coming out of his mouth are way too sexual for only having three bites of an empanada. And that leaves me thinking about Cade and sex. Are those the kinds of sounds he might make? My skin prickles with this new information and I have to shift in my chair. And why is Jenna's baking the thing that's managing to get this reaction? Another wave of jealousy rolls over me.

"She knows that, but I think she went into this with illusions of grandeur. She hadn't really realized the amount of work it would take."

"She should be happy we're willing to be in charge of it then." Cade licks the crumbs from his lips and I nearly faint. Who knew watching him eat could be an orgasmic experience?

"Not exactly. She said if we wanted to be in charge, then she quits." I wait for the reaction I'm sure Cade's going to have; he does not disappoint.

"Quits?" His hazel eyes go wide and then he leans back in his chair, laughter thudding out of him. "We should be so lucky. If she quits, then we can do it on our own."

I get an unexpected shiver of excitement. "You'd want to do that?"

"Do you still want your Harvest Festival?" He's serious, popping the last bite of his snack into his mouth and waiting for my answer.

"I really want a Harvest Festival," I confess, even if it makes me sound ridiculous. I should ask for a pony, too.

"We should eventually try to fix things with Molly, though. Don't want to ruin your friendship." There's that grin again.

"I don't think Molly and I were ever really going to be best buddies. But it might be easier to get the community part of this together with her help. Do you want to come with me to her house tomorrow to try to smooth things over?" I imagine waltzing into Molly's house with the extra protection of Cade by my side and get another little shiver.

"We can't tomorrow. We're floating."

I blink. "On the river? No one told me that."

I can see the moment Cade realizes he's said too much. He looks hurt *for* me, wincing a bit as he tries to figure out what to say next. They've planned something without me— or, really, Charlie has. Summertime is made for hot days spent on the river in an inner tube, and normally I'd be on the guest list. Not this time, I guess.

"Did Charlie forget to tell you? I'm sure it slipped his mind what with all the balls he's been juggling lately."

It's a good excuse, one I would normally buy if Charlie wasn't actually distracted by a certain chef and more than her skills in the kitchen. I've made it clear I don't like her, and he's made it clear he does. Even more clear today, if that's possible.

"Why don't I pick you up at eleven? Can you take a day off?"

"Cade, you don't have to—"

He silences me with a raise of a hand. "I want to. And everyone else will be expecting you to be there. Come with me."

I know he doesn't mean *with* him. But the idea of it sways me a little, and Cade pounces when he sees I'm weakening. "I'm sure there'll be ice cream after."

How can I say no to that?

## 19

*Cade*

My palms sweat the entire drive to Faith's house. I haven't told anyone I've invited her. Could I have casually slipped that nugget into conversation at family dinner last night? Sure. But then I would have had to deal with Charlie and whatever's made him decide Faith shouldn't be part of this excursion. I'd have had to put up with the questioning looks from my great-aunts and the rest of my family too. Working together on the mill doesn't mean inviting her to join me somewhere in her bathing suit. It also doesn't mean getting overly excited about the thought of that bathing suit, especially if I'm not sure I can keep that to myself. So I kept shoveling fried chicken into my mouth until Chance finally asked if I was trying to save up for the winter. I had eaten a whole chicken by that point, but being teased for my gluttony sure beat the alternative, because my sin these days is pure, unadulterated lust.

Faith comes skipping out her front door and down the walkway to my car. She's never in a bad mood, never without that blinding smile, and I've been working overtime to make sure I get my share of them. She waves and motions for me to pop the trunk. I stalk her movements through the rearview mirror as she wrestles her inner tube and cooler in there. Then she opens the passenger side door and slides back into the scene of the crime. Only she doesn't remember any of it; it's just me reliving her lips on mine.

"What?" Faith gives me a puzzled look.

"Huh?" I break eye contact and look out the windshield before I can say anything stupid. More stupid.

"You were making a weird face. Do I have crumbs on my chin or something?" Faith takes a swipe at her mouth with her hand.

"No."

"I brought too much beer, I think." The freckles on her nose crinkle as she talks.

"No such thing." I put the car in reverse and make a show of my driving skills. I certainly don't focus on the sprinkle of freckles I've noticed on Faith's thigh where her cut-off jeans stop and all that skin begins. My fingers itch to make their way over the console and touch her, slide up that thigh past the hem of those shorts and—

"Did you tell Charlie I was coming?"

"Charlie?" I don't need my brother interrupting my fantasy.

"There's maybe a reason he didn't invite me himself." The sadness in Faith's voice cuts me to the quick. Fuck my brother for making her feel like that. She's been nothing but loyal to Charlie for years and he's not doing the same for her.

"Well, *I* invited you. It wouldn't be a float trip without you. Let me worry about Charlie."

And my brother is definitely something to worry about if the look he gives me when I walk up with Faith is any indication. Charlie's glare could kill a lesser man and it's aimed directly at me. I shrug it off and try to act like nothing's wrong, but the general mood is a little cold when we all end up standing around trying to figure out the new lay of the land. Charlie's brought Jenna, and he's fawning all over her. It's plain to see he's interested in her in a way that could jeopardize the business. My decision to bring Faith with me doesn't go unnoticed, but it isn't the most interesting thing happening here. Not by a long shot.

Until she asks for my help with her sunscreen.

"Can you make sure I didn't miss any spots?" It's inno-cent enough, but I've already had to count to one hundred when Faith shucked off her shorts and tank top. Underneath was a red checkered bikini that I'm sure I've seen before, only today it's like I'm seeing it for the first time somehow. There's no hiding the curves Faith normally keeps under her overalls. I nearly choked on my own tongue when she leaned over to grab something out of her bag. Maybe all that sweetness isn't supposed to be sexy, but someone should really tell that to the unfortunate bulge in my swim trunks.

I clear my throat and take the bottle of sunscreen from Faith's outstretched hand; our fingers brush the slightest bit, and I know if that tiny bit of contact has my body winding tight, rubbing my palms all over her is going to give me a heart attack. She turns her back to me and moves her hair off her shoulders. There are more freckles there, ones that seem almost secret. You have to be close to Faith to see these, and I want to slide my tongue there, almost sure she'll taste like cinnamon and sugar. I squirt some lotion into the palm of my hand and try to warm it up a bit. There is nothing worse than having cold sunscreen slathered on you. Well, maybe there are worse things—my brothers all watching me as I try to pretend rubbing lotion into Faith's skin is as sexy as a visit to your grandmother's house, for example. It turns out that's much worse.

I can feel their eyes on me as I slide a finger underneath the strap of Faith's suit and make sure the lotion covers all of her. Her shoulders rise and fall as she breathes, and when I make another pass underneath the clasp in the back, goose bumps rise on her perfect skin.

"Is the lotion too cold?" I'm too close to her, my question nearly in her ear.

"No." Faith's voice is breathy and soft. "Did you get everything?"

"I think so." I want to spin her around and kiss her full on the mouth. I want to come up with a reason to keep my hands on her.

"Thank you." She turns her head, and she's close enough for me to notice the pink of her cheeks and the way her lashes fan out when she closes her eyes for a second.

I make myself take two steps back. "We should get in the water. Don't want it to be too late when we get home." It's the dumbest excuse ever. It's ten in the morning, for Pete's sake. We have plenty of time to float and be back before lunch. I take a look at my gobsmacked brothers standing on the river bank. Charlie's face is a mix of confusion and irritation. There's no way I won't be getting an earful about Faith and my *thorough application of sun cream* later. He'll probably try to dunk me, too, once we're out in deep enough water.

But I can't say I feel that much remorse, because no matter what Charlie decides to dish out, I'm willing to take it. He can try to drown me and this morning will still have been worth it.

## 20

*Faith*

Well, today wasn't going exactly the way I had imagined. Yes, the butterflies I had anticipated in my stomach every time Cade looked my way were as predictable as ever, but the rest of the day's events were far from it. Charlie has basically ignored me since I showed up, and I wasn't sure if that was because I had arrived with his younger brother or because he was too busy undressing Jenna with his eyes to take the time to do much else. It didn't take much effort to imagine Jenna naked in the tiny bikini she was wearing. Again, that rotten jealousy reared its head, and I tried to remember to be grateful Jenna had agreed to work with Charlie. That restaurant needs a world-class chef, and she has the chops. Their grand opening is coming up soon, and I'm not going to do anything that might make Jenna upset.

I kept myself busy trying to enjoy the water. The river was cold enough to take the sting out of a hot day, and every time I looked over at Cade, he'd been looking back at me.

"You need another beer?" It was hard to listen to what Cade was asking when his bare chest kept distracting me.

"If you can reach the cooler." We were in our usual loose pattern of bodies, the occasional arm or leg slung over someone else's inner tube to keep them close for a minute.

"For you I can." A response like that went straight to my heart, and the way Lily and Hadley bent their heads together let me know they heard it too.

Hadley had been nice enough to invite us all to her and Cooper's house for lunch once we dragged ourselves up the muddy river bank. Floating shouldn't get you filthy, but I always ended up covered in grit and mud. But I forgot all about the sand in my bikini bottoms when Jenna informed us all that she and Charlie had more planned for the afternoon. And can you guess what he'd invited her to do, right after freezing me out of the float trip? Charlie Allen was taking her blueberry picking. Of all things, he had to choose the one thing he and I always did together. It had burned me up something fierce to think of the two of them over at Miller's farm, filling those plastic buckets with handful after handful of ripe fruit. I bit my tongue, but wasn't the least bit sad when Lily and Hadley horned in on those plans. I thought I saw a little curl of Jenna's lip when she realized her time with Charlie was going to become even more extended family time, but she at least had the good sense to pretend it didn't bother her.

Charlie, on the other hand, was like the worst kind of toddler. He had made up some excuse about the two of them needing to get some work done, trying first to get out of lunch and then making it impossible for us to come along to Miller's. But I'm not the only one making faces when Charlie moons over Jenna—and he's definitely mooning. It's worse than I've ever seen him and I can't say I understand his choices. The only plus side? He hasn't really had time to notice me mooning over Cade.

"That is not exactly what I was expecting." I follow the path of Hadley's interested stare to find Charlie closer than he needs to be to Jenna. Again. He might think it looks like he's trying to teach her how to pick blueberries—something that doesn't need much in the way of explanation, by the way—but his hands are nowhere near the bushes.

"None of the other boys are going to be able to ignore that for long." Lily frowns. Discontent between the brothers is something no one wants, especially now that they're running a business together. The parts may be separate, but the restaurant and distillery need to coordinate, and Chance and Cade have their roles to play, too. Charlie is threatening to tip that delicate balance with his Jenna shenanigans.

"You pick way faster than I do." Cade's voice comes from directly behind me. Hadley and Lily get very interested in the contents of their plastic buckets.

"I'm a pro." I am a farmer, after all, even if that really doesn't apply to what we're doing here. "Want me to show you how to get the ripe ones quicker?" *Now who's pretending to teach someone something they already know?*

"Sure." Cade steps in close enough for me to smell him, and I try to be discreet about filling my lungs with that now familiar scent. *Why does he have to smell so good?* I'm going to end up with my nose buried in the front of his shirt here in a minute if I don't control myself.

"If they're really ready you can almost run your hand over the branch." I demonstrate with my bucket poised under the cascade of fruit I'm about to unleash. "Like this. See?"

Of course Cade sees, and, of course, he knows this already. He's been blueberry picking for as long as I have, and he's even had the added benefit of going with Sadie and Mae. Those ladies are jam-making machines in the summer, and I know for a fact they used to press the boys into service when it came to picking. Cade can probably clear a strawberry patch faster than me and has picked his fair share of peaches. Charlie used to complain about having to miss bike rides and baseball games when it was time to help his great-aunts. Not that he was complaining when it came time to eat blueberry pie, mind you. I cast a glance at Charlie and Jenna smiling at each other as they work and get that pang in my heart again.

"What's that all about, do you think?" Cade asks, and I get a different kind of pang when I look at his chiseled jaw. Biting him would be completely out of line, but that doesn't keep me from considering it. His hand comes up near mine and stays there.

"He's nothing if not predictable." I focus on the blueberry bush. Charlie's known for his questionable choices in women. At least this time the woman in question seems sane, even if his sense of professional boundaries doesn't.

"Well, he can't pull his 'love 'em and leave 'em' routine with Jenna. We don't need any burned bridges there." Cade's fingers almost touch mine, and the way he's looking at me has me caring less and less about Charlie and Jenna. "Let me try your trick."

We work side by side for the next hour until we've got more blueberries than we'll ever be able to eat. I've been sampling as I go so I've already had more than my daily allotment of blueberries.

"Should we have weighed Faith before y'all started?" This is Mr. Miller's favorite joke, and he's been telling it since I was five. "We charge by the pound, you know, and I'm betting Faith here's gained an extra pound or two since she started picking."

Normally I laugh right along with everyone else, but

today I don't want to be called out for anything that makes me look like the immature tomboy I know I am. I try to shake off the feeling of being the butt of the joke, but I can't help but notice how funny Jenna seems to find that particular comment.

"Then you should've weighed me too." Cade's hand comes to rest on the small of my back. "Because you could probably add an extra pound or three to my total. Part of the fun of picking is sampling."

The confessions from the rest of our group start to roll in, but I barely hear a thing. I'm only aware of the whoosh of air that rushes through my ears when I look at Cade and his big, goofy grin. He gives me an awkward side hug and then releases me. On our way back to the car, he bumps me a bit every now and then, his arm grazing mine. I want more than anything for his hand to reach out and capture mine, but that doesn't happen, and I'm too timid to take the risk of twining my purple and magenta stained fingers with his.

It only takes a minute for the entire interior of the car to smell like blueberries. At Miller's there's nothing fancy; the berries get poured into regular plastic grocery bags for the ride home and they bounce around the backseat. There are a few smells that always make me think of summer: honeysuckle, strawberries, ballpark hotdogs. But I know from now on whenever I smell blueberries I'm going to be thinking of Cade. I sneak glances at him as he drives, his face a little pink on the bridge of his nose from too much sun today. He catches me looking and gives me a little half-smile, keeping his eyes on the road.

"I'll help you bring these in." Before I can protest, he's out of the car and coming around to my side. He opens the door for me—something not many men insist on doing for a tomboy who's built her reputation on being self-sufficient —and grabs the largest bag of berries.

"I can carry them," I tell him even as I'm enjoying having Cade take care of me a little. It's nice in a way I wouldn't have expected. I'm more than capable and he knows this, but he's helping me anyway.

When we get to the door of my tiny little house, there isn't enough room for the both of us on the front stoop. One day I'll have a house with a great front porch for sitting, but for now I've only got this little patch of concrete with barely enough space for two grown ups and a few bags of blueberries.

"Thank you for an interesting day."

Cade laughs that perfect laugh of his, and I feel it everywhere. "That's one word for it." He runs his free hand through his hair and errant strands stay standing. "I'm really glad you came with me."

There it is again—the idea of an us. I try not to put too much hope on that, but my heart swells a little all the same.

"I can take these." I shift my bag of berries and end up closer to him. We jostle a bit; I reach for the bag he's holding and our hands fumble together to make the exchange. That one touch is like lightning, and I know he feels it too when he lowers his eyes to meet mine. This time I can read the look he gives me perfectly.

Lust.

Blueberries roll all over the stoop as Cade drops his bag and reaches for me. His hands grasp my face and slide into my hair as his mouth meets mine. Never before have I understood what people mean when they say their knees go weak, but right now I absolutely get it. My entire body turns to jelly as I press against Cade, my bag of blueberries bumping against his sun-kissed thigh as I try to get as close as humanly possible to him. I only break contact to ask if he wants to come inside. It surprises even me, but Cade doesn't hesitate. He just nods and waits while I open the door, close enough for me to still feel the heat of his chest on my back.

## 21

*Cade*

I'm inside Faith's house. If I didn't cross a line out on the porch, I've certainly crossed it now, because I didn't come in here for a cup of coffee. No sir, I came in here with the intention of finishing what we started outside. The two seconds I spend not kissing Faith doesn't clear my head in the slightest and doesn't make me think twice about what I've done or what I'm about to do. The idea that Charlie might kill me dances around the edges of my brain, but I don't let it take root. I push it down and concentrate on getting my hands on Faith again. This time she's stone cold sober and fully aware of what we're doing. This might be terrible for the goal of brotherly love, and it might not be great for keeping Faith at arm's length in the long run, but I've been doing a shitty job of both of those things for a little while now.

And she feels too good in my arms to stop.

I nearly take the screen door off its hinges as we tumble inside. Faith's house is tiny, but there's not a thing out of place. I spend exactly one second looking around and then I reach for her again. She comes willingly, letting me pull her close and start kissing her again. Faith tastes like blueberries, sweet and tart at the same time, and I can't stop myself from moving from her mouth to taste the rest of her. We'd all taken two minute showers at Cooper and Hadley's after lunch, but Faith's still got a hint of coconut-scented sunscreen on her neck. I slide my nose along her throat and am rewarded with the sexiest little moan. Good Lord, Faith Baker has me turned on like never before from five minutes of a high school make-out session. Going any further is going to be the death of me.

Faith's hands roam up my back, first over the fabric of my T-shirt and then, as she gets a little bolder, underneath. Her palms are warm and her touch gentle, but she isn't timid. She grabs the hem of my shirt and lifts it over my head, touching me like she's got a right to. It's a side of Faith I had never expected to see, and as her hands move over my chest and down to the waistband of my shorts, I'm not sure I can ever go back to before this moment right now. But that means she likely won't be able to either.

"Wait." I bring my hands to my sides and make myself take a step back. "What are we doing?"

Faith's lips are swollen from my kisses, her cheeks flushed. She looks almost drunk, her eyes still hazy, the lids low.

"Is this... Is this something you want?" She's told me, but I need her to say it again, to say it now when she's still able to change her mind.

"You... You don't?" Faith's mouth turns down a little and she lowers her eyes. "Of course you don't."

"I've wanted this for as long as I can remember."

That gets her. Her mouth opens and closes and she stares at me, blinking.

"Faith, you can call the shots here, but I want this more than I should." I'm standing shirtless in the living room of Faith's house, and I figure I've got nothing to lose. "And I'm pretty sure you want it too because you've already told me."

Her brow furrows. "No, I haven't."

"You have. The night I stayed here. In the car you told me everything."

"Everything?" Faith squeaks. "What did I say exactly?"

"That you thought I was smart and handsome. You told me that a few times." I can't keep from smiling a bit, but I try to keep the teasing out of my voice. Now isn't the time to make Faith self-conscious.

"This is a nightmare. All this time and you never said anything? Why didn't you tell me that next morning? Why didn't you let me know I'd made a fool of myself in the car? You told Charlie, didn't you? Y'all have been laughing about it for weeks now." Faith is clearly mortified and looking like she might run and lock herself in her bedroom any second now. That's not how I want this to end, so I go ahead and blurt the rest out before she can flee the scene.

"No! It's not like that, Faith. I would never tell Charlie anything about what happens with us." I don't mention that telling my brother would result in a fist fight long before anyone would be laughing. "And you kissed me, Faith. The next morning you didn't remember, but I haven't been able to forget. Having to see you every damn day in those overalls is killing me. We can stop, but it isn't going to keep me from thinking about you."

"You like my overalls?" Faith's voice is a whisper.

"Those overalls are about the sexiest thing I've ever seen.

Except maybe that bathing suit you had on earlier today. I think everything about you is...perfect."

"Perfect?" There's a tremble in her voice.

"Absolutely. But I want to be sure this is what you want too. I don't want—" I don't get to finish any of that because Faith starts walking toward me, lifting the hem of her shirt and pulling it over her head. She chucks it on the floor and reaches down to unbutton her shorts. I'm already speechless at the sight of her.

"Can we get back to what we were doing before you decided to turn this into a contract negotiation?" Faith shimmies out of her cutoffs and I nod. Whatever she asks me now I'm going to say yes.

"Where were we, exactly?" My fingers are already itching to slide all over the exposed skin of her belly.

"Well, you weren't standing all the way over there."

I'm pressed up against her before she can say another word. I want to touch every inch of her, and Faith isn't exactly keeping her hands to herself. We stumble through the living room, a tangle of arms and legs, our mouths fused together. If I had been trying to slow things down earlier, it didn't work, and I'm not at all mad about it.

"Should we go—" Faith's words get swallowed up in another blistering kiss. "Bedroom," she manages to pant out.

We knock plenty of things over on our way down the hallway but that doesn't slow us down. Faith doesn't even seem to notice the framed photo that comes crashing down when we end up pressed against the wall of her tiny little hallway. You'd think we'd be able to make it five feet without needing to stop, but Faith's hand's made its way down the front of my shorts, making it impossible for me to do anything but groan. I manage to get her bra off despite the lack of blood going anywhere near my brain, and pull a nipple in between my teeth as she strokes me. I am nowhere near the player my brothers are, and Faith's hands are about to do me in. There is no way I'm going to let things end before they even have a chance to get started. Reluctantly, I pull away. Faith's confused eyes meet mine.

"Let's make sure you're good and warmed up first."

_____

## 22

_Faith_

*We are really doing this. Actually doing this. Cade Allen is in my bedroom. I am nearly naked, and Cade Allen is in my bedroom.* My brain is having trouble processing all of this. It doesn't help that Cade's abs have all sorts of things short circuiting when it comes to straight thinking. I have spent too many summers to count looking at those washboard abs and dreaming about what they might feel like if I got a second to run my fingers over them. I'm getting my answer now and then some, because I am touching way more than Cade's abs as we stumble down the hallway.

He groans deep and low as I slide my hand past the waistband of his shorts. I'm trying to be forward here—I'm not exactly inexperienced, but there's no one in the world who would see the metaphorical notches on my bedpost and assume I was a sex goddess. Still, Cade doesn't seem to be complaining when I take his erection in my hand and give him a stroke. On the contrary, he stops moving and his eyes nearly roll back in his head. I debate other options. Why did I never listen when my sisters were dissecting all their sexual exploits? It had seemed in bad taste to get all that information about some poor boy who had made the mistake of sleeping with one of my gossipy sisters, and, besides, it made it pretty difficult to play baseball without blushing once you knew specifics about what everyone was packing in their pants.

But from the sounds Cade's making and the look on his face, I'm doing fine. He's got his head leaned back against the wall, eyes shut tight. His hips rock a bit with the motion of my hand. I could look at his face forever, I think—the square jaw and the slight bump on the bridge of his nose. His eyes snap open, and his hands move to the clasp of my bra. He's quick to get it off me and it disappears somewhere down the hall back toward the living room. I'm not entirely prepared for the sensation of Cade's mouth on me. He has to bend down to reach my breasts, twisting so I don't lose my grip. The sting of his teeth on my nipple has me gasping at first, but then his tongue laves the spot and I'm the one squeezing my eyes shut. When he pulls away I whimper—a sound I don't recall ever making before.

"Let's make sure you're good and warmed up first." Cade's eyes are full of nothing but want and his hand is sliding low down my belly.

I'm feeling more than a little warmed up, but I'm not about to stop whatever Cade has in mind. He takes my hand and nearly tows me down the hall, straight to my bedroom and onto the pristine white sheets of my bed. And I do mean pristine because, first of all, while I might work in the dirt all day, I like my living space to be spic and span, and secondly, there hasn't been a man in this bed since I made the mistake of trying to date Clayton Harris three years ago. I have been in the dry spell to end all dry spells. And now, somehow, I have Cade Allen in my bedroom.

He gets me on my back in no time, sliding his body over mine. I involuntarily arch up, still wanting to be skin to skin with him even if it means contorting myself. Cade plants a line of kisses down my body, ending up with his lips grazing the elastic of my panties. He nuzzles me, and my hips shoot off the bed.

Cade's chuckle doesn't do much to help me relax. He takes his time kissing the inside of my thighs, always stopping just far enough away from my center to have me squirming. When he eases my panties down, I let him, but I can already feel myself tensing up.

"You don't have to do that."

Cade looks up from between my legs. "This is not a have to; this is a want to. A want to *very* much."

I gulp.

Cade's mouth comes down on me and my hips shoot up again. I press my back against the mattress and try to take deep breaths. "You don't have to keep going."

"Do you not... Do you not like oral?" Cade's face is still between my legs, his expression bewildered. "It's okay if you don't, I just—"

"It's been my experience that men don't really like doing it." I boost myself up on my elbows and look down at Cade. He's on his knees at the foot of the bed, still close enough for me to feel his breath on me every time he exhales.

"Seriously? People have seen this pussy right here and haven't wanted to camp out for a bit?"

My face flames.

"Faith, I don't know what kind of idiots you've been dating, but I like doing this a lot and I think you'd be doing me a disservice by not giving me a chance to change your mind." He's serious, and despite the fact that he's got his face in my crotch, I decide to believe him. *He said I was perfect.*

"I've never been able to finish this way." It's more information than I'd like to give him, but he should know in advance, I figure.

"That's because it takes more than thirty seconds. Trust me, you'll come."

I'm not used to someone being so...blunt about it. The men I've been with haven't been much for talking, and the sex has always been fine, but never anything to write home about. I take a deep breath and lay back down. "Okay, but don't be surprised if this doesn't work."

"Challenge accepted." Cade grips my thighs and pulls me to the end of the bed, throwing my legs over his shoulders. I choose not to entertain my normal level of mortification and instead close my eyes and start counting. Cade's right; my previous partners have always quit before I get to thirty.

"God, Faith, you taste so good."

There's another difference between Cade and the tiny number of men before him—Cade is a talker. And a moaner. The sounds he's making are not the sounds a man makes when he's doing a chore he hates. Not at all. And I find myself moving, grinding an embarrassing amount on Cade's face. Instead of making him run screaming from my bedroom, this only seems to make him more excited.

"Just like that, Faith. Ride my face, baby."

I would not have pegged Cade for a dirty talker, but that's what seems to be happening. The first time, it surprises me, but the second time? The second time it turns me on enough to have me fisting the sheets. And something amazing is happening to my body. I've had orgasms before, or, at least, that's what I tell people. But the sensation I'm having now isn't like any of that. I've long since stopped counting in my head—there's no room for that now—and the noises coming out of my mouth are not of the ladylike variety. My toes are literally curling, my heels digging into Cade's back.

I can feel something building deep inside me, and when it finally breaks free, I realize for the first time in my life what all the fuss is about. No wonder people do all sorts of crazy things to get this kind of high again! If you told me right now, as I'm seeing stars behind my eyelids, that I could float out of this bedroom, I would believe you. The orgasm crashes over me in waves and for a minute I can't even feel my feet. Cade doesn't stop, even when it's more than obvious I'm the loser in our bet. Although I'd never call this losing.

Cade moves back a bit and lets my legs slide off his shoulders. They dangle off the end of the bed, and I don't bother pulling my knees together the way I would have in the past. Cade's already seen plenty, and he seems more than happy with the view. I try to slow my breathing and catch my breath as Cade's body comes up over mine.

"See?" It's more a statement of fact than anything else.

I let out one long exhale. "Holy shit."

Cade's face moves back from mine a fraction and his eyes widen. "Faith, did you just cuss?"

I did. I most certainly did. And with good reason. A revelation like that deserves something monumental.

Cade's smile is a mile wide. "If you thought that was good, wait until you see my next move."

I can hardly wait.

## 23

*Cade*

The front stoop is a mess. I'm still whistling, though, as I pick up the spilled blueberries. It's a bitch to have to squat down and rescue each berry one by one, but there isn't a better way to do it and save the fruit. Already the birds have been helping themselves, but there's plenty to go around, and the ones I'm putting back in the plastic bag only need a little rinse to be edible again.

Faith snuck out early. With any other woman I'd have taken that personally, but with a farmer, an early wake-up call is expected. She'd slid out of bed before the sun was up, leaving me a note about how to work the coffee maker and not to worry about the mess. We did destroy her house a little. Two people with one singular goal of getting naked proved to be too much for this little place. Still, I'm mentally patting myself on the back as I gather up the blueberries and head back into the house. I'm tired, but in a good way, and I've still got the smile on my face from last night.

I'd made Faith Baker cuss. More than once.

I'm pretty sure that makes me some kind of demigod. It's

bragging rights for sure; that is, if I was prone to bragging. And if I had anyone to tell. I frown a little at this. Knowing I'm going to have to keep this from Charlie takes a little of the shine off my good mood. My other brothers are probably best left in the dark as well. No need to have them knowing something they can't share. Secrets like that tend to have a life of their own, and I don't want to put Cooper and Chance in the middle of anything. Faith either, but I know it's too late for that.

"You're up." Faith sounds surprised. She comes into the kitchen carrying a paper-wrapped package. "Dan Rayborn gave me some bacon to try." In that moment I'm not sure if it's still the post-sex glow or the promise of smoked meat, but Faith has never looked more beautiful.

"That'll go great with the pancakes I'm about to make you. Where do you keep your flour?"

"You're making breakfast?" Faith doesn't sound as excited as I'd like.

"Sure. Aren't you hungry?" I could mention something cheesy about how she must have worked up an appetite after last night, but I doubt Faith would find that funny. It took me a while to get her to relax, and I don't want to squander that on stupid jokes.

"I am, I just thought you might not want to stick around."

"Do you want me to go?" I wasn't expecting to be kicked out so early this morning, but maybe Faith needs her space.

"No, I guess I'm not used to having someone want to do the morning thing. I'm not even all that used to the sleep-over, if I'm being honest."

I get another flash of anger. I had a few of those last night as I realized how awful the guys Faith's been with really are. Selfish and self-centered are the nicest words I can muster this morning for more than one man who wasn't even interested in Faith's pleasure or feelings. They weren't making her come or making her breakfast. *Assholes*.

"Do you actually know how to make pancakes?" Faith doesn't look convinced.

"Of course, I used to make them for my mom all the time when I lived at home. Pancakes are easy."

"Was that after your parents got divorced?" It's a tricky subject for me, but I can't expect Faith to know that. She and Charlie must have talked about the divorce, but by then he was nearly out of the house.

"Yep. For a while there it was only me and my mom. She can't cook to save her life, so I learned a few things here and there so we wouldn't starve. Flour?" I try to get the conversation back to breakfast; I don't want to start dissecting my parents' divorce at seven in the morning. If I keep it light I won't have to tell Faith all the sordid details.

"It's over here." Faith pulls a container from the bank of cabinets behind her and hands it to me. "Did you make dinner too? For your mother?"

I concentrate on gathering ingredients so Faith can't see the warring emotions on my face. Thinking about the time after my father left for good is both painful and happy. My mother was free of him and, in theory, so was I. But by the time the divorce was over, there wasn't much left of the spunky, hilarious woman who had been my mother. That meant me stepping up and taking charge, being serious. None of my older brothers were around much, so I didn't have a choice. It was two years of my mother falling apart and me picking up the pieces. It's why I know how to make pancakes, but it's also why I know how to grocery shop like a pro and never miss paying the electric bill. It's how I know you can still hear someone crying even if they run the shower to drown out the noise.

"Sometimes."

"What would you make?" Faith gets a cup of coffee and sits at the little table. There's barely room for two, and I'm sure when I finally sit down across from her our knees will touch.

"Whatever she wanted." That really means whatever I could convince her to eat. My mother got awfully skinny when it was only the two of us. "I can make almost anything from a recipe."

"Impressive." Faith takes a sip of her coffee and looks out the kitchen window. She's got a fine view, but nothing like the one I've got at my house. And she's only got one mixing bowl and a smattering of wooden spoons. I doubt Faith does much cooking in here. "Can I help?"

"You just sit there and look pretty." I more than mean the pretty part, but Faith scowls a bit.

"You don't have to keep saying things like that." She actually rolls her eyes.

"You need to take 'have to' out of your vocabulary. I'm not doing anything here because I have to." I stop my measuring and sifting and give her a long look.

"It's a little over the top."

Again, Faith's words poke at my heart. How no one has been worshipping at the altar of Faith Baker is beyond me. "I think it's not nearly enough."

Faith shakes her head. She's uncomfortable with compliments, but that isn't going to keep me from giving them.

"I meant everything I said last night. Those weren't lines I was using to get you naked."

I'm not sure Faith is convinced, but she doesn't argue. "We can't tell Charlie, though."

The last person I want to talk about right now is my brother. "What's Charlie got to do with any of this?" I move away from the counter and squat down until I'm eye level with Faith. "He's the last thing I'm thinking about right now." And just like that I really have forgotten all about Charlie, because Faith is biting her bottom lip in a way that only makes me think of one thing. I'm not even thinking about blueberry pancakes, and I was pretty focused on those five minutes ago. Now I'm hungry for something else. I lean forward and give Faith the kiss she should have gotten this morning. The one I would have given her if we'd woken up still tangled together in her bedsheets.

Faith more than kisses me back, and I know we aren't going to be eating breakfast until maybe lunch time.

## 24

*Faith*

There is no way I'm going to be able to get through Sunday lunch without exploding. Probably not literally, but the secret I've been holding in keeps threatening to bust out of me at any second. Everyone else is having polite conversation, and all I can think about is Cade's head between my legs. Is that what everyone else has been experiencing for years? I look at the faces of my sisters and wonder if any of them have ever had sex in the shower. It turns out my tiny little bathroom isn't the best for maneuverability, but—

"What are you smiling about over there?" Hope's question silences the entire room.

"Me?" Maybe I should have at least pretended to be interested in whatever story Charity was telling.

"Yes, *you*. You've been goofy all afternoon, and you've barely eaten two bites." Hope points to my plate but I'm sure no one needed the extra help.

"I had a late breakfast." I'm not about to fill in any more details than that, although my face feels like it's on fire. I was almost certain when I walked into my parents' house today that everyone would be able to see something was different. My lips were still swollen from kissing Cade up until the absolute last second. I'm walking a little funny, too, and there's no way I'm explaining that to anyone. How can I be twenty-nine years old and have never really had an orgasm? I would have loved to have been able to talk to any of my sisters about the things I learned last night, but if I want to keep my relationship with Cade from Charlie, telling the world's worst gossips isn't the way to do it. Not that they would have been particularly understanding. They'd probably have howled with laughter that their little sister had taken a lifetime to figure out what they all probably realized in ninth grade.

"You still should try to eat, Faith. Your mama worked hard so you could fill that plate." My father's face is only slightly stern. He's probably wondering why I'm looking out the window all dreamy instead of being my usual self. I can always be counted on to listen intently and ask the right questions when it comes to conversation. I can't exactly tell him I've got too much sex on the brain to care about what kind of pie Mama made for dessert.

'Well, you and Faith did grow the vegetables." My mother smiles at my father. "Although I'm a little surprised you aren't interested in those potatoes, Faith. They're usually your favorite."

"I'm surprised Faith has time to grow anything." Connie's face tells me this is the setup for something I don't want to hear. "From what I've heard she's been pretty busy stealing the Historical Society from Molly Eagan."

"Oh, I heard about that too." Charity drags out the *oh* until it takes on a life of its own. "Molly was telling *everyone* at the last Junior League meeting." Her contribution to the discussion doesn't help me much.

"That doesn't sound like Faith." My mother swivels to look at me. Luckily, she doesn't know all the other out of character things I've been up to lately.

"It isn't like that. Cade and I decided Molly's leadership style was a little...overbearing. We suggested a few changes, that's all." I put some of my mother's potato casserole in my mouth to keep myself from saying anything more.

"That's not how Molly tells it. According to her, you and Cade kicked her out of her own group. Decided the two of you were going to be in charge of the mill thing on your own. She seemed pretty upset about it. It was her idea originally, and you took it away from her. What are you doing with the mill, anyway? It seems a little dumb to take on something that means more work for yourself. Isn't that mill falling apart?" Charity shrugs her shoulders and her blonde waves move with the motion.

"It sounds like a big waste of time, if you ask me." Connie would say that. She's not exactly the poster child for sticking with things. Hope nods her agreement.

"Girls, if Faith wants to pursue that, it isn't any of our business. And the Junior League meeting hardly seems the place for gossip." It has apparently been a long time since my mother has attended a Junior League meeting around here if that's what she thinks.

"It isn't our business so long as it doesn't interfere with our actual business." My father raises an eyebrow in my direction. I'm sure he'll tell me more about that once we're done with lunch and back to working.

"It won't, Daddy." As long as I can keep up with the things I need to do, he won't have anything to complain about. If I can keep it together long enough to get through the rest of this meal then I can do anything.

"I finally saw that new chef Charlie hired; no wonder

Faith's been trying to find something to fill her free time." Hope casually puts a bite of cornbread in her mouth and looks at me as she chews.

"What is that supposed to mean?" I know what she's implying, but I'm not about to let her get under my skin.

"I'm thinking he probably doesn't mind all those late nights so much." She waggles her perfect eyebrows at me.

"She's pretty then?" Connie's all ears, sitting up a little taller and nearly putting her elbows on the table.

"Let me put it this way..." Hope pauses to make sure we're all listening. "When she walked into Ham & Eggs there wasn't one man whose head didn't turn. I even thought I saw Henry looking up from the grill. She's very...distinctive."

I stifle a groan. Leave it to Hope to build Jenna up to be some sort of mythical goddess. "She's pretty but she's not..."

"She's more than pretty, Faith. She's *hot*. Almost dirty hot."

"Hope Baker, I think this is veering into not-reasonable-for-Sunday-lunch territory." My mother's rebuke is stern, but it does nothing to chastise my sister or keep her from talking.

"She's got that kind of bad girl thing going on—tight pants and black T-shirts. She looks like she rides a motor-cycle or something. No wonder Charlie's not helping with the Historical Society crap—he's busy with his own real life pin-up girl."

"Ohhhh." Connie leans back in her chair and ignores the less than pleased glances from both our parents. "It would be hard to compete with that. Not that Faith's in any kind of a competition with her, really. I think what that chef's offering probably beats fishing any day."

"Easily," Charity confirms and all but winks at my other sisters. Once again I feel like I'm about five years old.

"If y'all will excuse me for a minute." I let the legs of my chair scrape as loudly as they want to when I get up from the table. I don't even bother waiting for Daddy to stand up or for the rest of my family to see the anger on my face. I march off to the half bath down the hall and lock the door behind me.

I can only stall for so long in here before I'll need to go back out and face everyone with a somewhat calm and collected appearance. I splash a little water on my face and run my wrists under the tap. I've never known how to deal with the things my sisters say. It's always seemed like they don't fight fair, and I never understood the rules anyway. With boys, it was always easy—there weren't any hidden meanings or traps. But even now I'm not sure if my sisters were trying to hurt me or merely making conversation. Either way, I don't want to spend the time to figure it out.

My phone buzzes in my pocket and I fish it out, almost certain it's going to be a customer with an update to their vegetable order. Always being available is one of the things I try to use to our advantage. I'm not a nine-to-five customer service rep, I'm your neighbor down the street. If you end up deciding you need zucchini on Sunday night for Monday's lunch service, I do my best to make that happen. I can't always move mountains, but at least it looks like I'm trying. But it isn't a customer.

It's Cade.

*Still thinking about you, beautiful.*

Take that, mean girls.

## 25

*Cade*

I have definitely opened Pandora's box. If I thought finally getting close enough to Faith would help to cool some of the feelings I was having, I was dead wrong. It doesn't hurt that she's even better than I could have imagined. No wonder Charlie claimed her as his best friend years and years ago. I would have done that myself had I realized then how awesome she is. I've always liked the outside, but Faith's not just a pretty face. She's smart and funny, helpful and determined. I was already spending too much of my day thinking about her, and now there's no way I can stop.

Seeing her Monday morning isn't exactly an accident. I know she's coming to the restaurant with the vegetable delivery. Can I help it if my run takes me right by there? I pretend I can't and even pretend I've forgotten my Camelback and have to stop for water. Faith smiles at me and ducks her head, and for a second I think Charlie might notice something's up, but he's so far in his own little world he barely notices Faith at all. That makes me bold enough to follow her out to her truck and pull her back behind the building.

"Hey." I'm grinning so much my face hurts.

"Hey," she whispers back, and I press her up against the wall and kiss her hard. It's already promising to be a hot day, and I entertain the fantasy of skipping work and convincing Faith to go down to the river for a swim. I let my hands roam over her, not caring about the obvious danger of this location. She's bolder than I would have expected, too, and when we finally break apart we're both panting.

"I have to go back to work," Faith tells me, but then starts kissing me again.

It's at least two minutes later when I answer her. "Me too." Neither of us lets that stop us, though, and when she finally gets in her truck I have to take the long way home so no one notices the hard-on I'm sporting.

I feel like an ass an hour later when Chance and Cooper convince me we have to have a talk with Charlie about Jenna. It's pretty hard not to feel like a hypocrite when we remind him the chef is supposed to be off-limits. I'm pretty sure the spot out back where I was kissing Faith is still warm as Charlie yells at us to mind our own business. Turns out I'm not so good at honoring my off-limits agreements either.

He's still mad as a hornet when he catches me up at the distillery. I'm finishing up some paperwork and sitting at the bar when Charlie comes up next to me and slams his hand down on the worn wood of the bar top. I jump.

"What the hell was that for?"

"We need to talk." He sits on the stool next to me and gives me a menacing stare. "You had a lot of nerve bringing Faith the other day."

"*I* had a lot of nerve? I mentioned it to Faith and figured you hadn't gotten around to inviting her yet. You didn't tell me it was a secret, and you never clued me in that I was supposed to keep Faith away so you could better woo Jenna. Not that I'd help you with that anyway." I turn my eyes back to my computer screen.

"You're supposed to be helping her with business stuff, not rubbing your hands all over her." I know exactly what Charlie's talking about.

"I *am* helping her with business stuff. I'm not allowed to make sure she doesn't get a sunburn? She asked me to put sunscreen on her and I did. You think you should have done it for her or something? You were pretty busy, if I recall." I try to turn things back around so Charlie's the bad guy. He's the one potentially ruining things, right? My sins are small in comparison.

"Cut it out, Cade. Faith isn't the kind of girl you can play with. Whatever you're thinking, stop thinking it." Charlie's nostrils flare.

"You're only mad because we told you how we felt about you and Jenna. Don't act like this is about me spending time with Faith." The best way out of this is to plead ignorance, so I keep up the charade. "You're the one who told me to help her. It's not like you've been paying much attention to her anyway."

Charlie stews for a minute, and I think he might be about to leave me alone when he gives me a little bit of a shove. "I'm not messing around, Cade."

"Neither am I. Faith's not your property. You don't get to decide who she hangs out with. She's a grown woman who can make her own decisions." I think about shoving him back, but getting in a fist fight inside the distillery would be a bad idea. Getting in a fist fight *anywhere* would get us both in trouble with Mae and Sadie, but breaking a bunch of things in here would get us in deep with Cooper and

Chance. Being able to mentally calculate the cost of every breakable thing in here helps me keep my hands to myself.

"She might be grown, but she's sweet, naive. I don't want you messing with that. I've had a hard enough time keeping other guys from hassling her. I don't need my own brother taking advantage of her."

"You've told other guys to leave her alone? Does Faith know that?" No wonder all the guys who've been interested in her are losers. She would be livid. "She's got a father, Charlie, she doesn't need another one."

He scowls at this, but he's already winding down. Now that he's gotten some of the anger out, even if it's misplaced, he seems a little better. "Just cool it with her, okay?"

I don't answer because I don't want to further the lie. If Charlie's upset about the way I touched Faith at the river, then he'd see red if he found out I spent the night. But Faith isn't fragile the way he thinks she is, and from what I can tell, it's about time she got to make some choices for herself. Well past time.

## 26

*Faith*

"So where are you so far?"

Chance's question should bring me back to focusing, but it does little to make me stop thinking about Cade's bare chest. Even here in one of the conference rooms at Allen Brothers, I've got sex on the brain. I should be extra careful not to look like I'm drooling all over this impressive barn wood table.

"I can answer that." In reality, Cade's got on one of his crisp button downs, the sleeves rolled up to the forearms. I can just as easily let my eyes settle there and be fine with the view.

"Anything to add, Faith?"

Cade must have been talking, but other than watching his mouth move, I don't think I've heard a word. That's not going to be great for convincing Chance to help us with the preservation of the mill. I'm not supposed to be a silent partner, and I'm not supposed to be a distracted one either.

"I guess not." There, three words. Cade smiles at me, and

I'm pretty sure those will be the only words I can manage to get out. I try to bring my sex-addled mind back to reality. I'm in a meeting, not my bedroom. I'm trying to do good for the community, not focus on the way Cade's long fingers look wrapped around that ball point pen. But they do look good, especially when I think about them—

"And it was Molly's idea to do some kind of event, but I'm not sure when we're going to get to that point. I'm thinking if we focus on the mill and plan our mission on saving that one building in particular, we'll stand a better chance of being successful." Cade swivels a bit in his chair.

"What?" That does bring me back to reality. "We'd focus only on the mill?"

"To start," Cade clarifies. "That would give the Historical Society a focus. I'm working on setting up the 501(c)(3) so we can legally be a not-for-profit, but that's slow going. I'm not sure if we can get everything together in time to have a festival this year, Faith." The way he says my name does me in a little. It's softer than usual, and to my ears almost sounds like a pet name. I'm hoping it doesn't sound that way to his brother, though, because Chance doesn't need to have even an inkling of any of that.

"Why didn't you tell me this before?" My question gets a raised eyebrow from Cade. We haven't been doing much talking lately. Even if he had tried to tell me about his work on saving the mill, I probably would have been listening with only one ear. The other one would have been busy listening to Cade's heart beat in his chest and thinking about how to convince him to stay the night.

"I did, but we need to go over it again for Chance anyway. Do you think Molly's going to be a no-show?" Cade changes the subject before I can reveal how little I know about what he's been doing.

"She hasn't returned any of my calls, and to hear my sisters tell it, she told everyone in Junior League that you and I stole the Historical Society from her." I scrunch my face up like I've just had a spoonful of cough syrup. "I doubt she's coming today."

"We should still try to keep her involved. She'll cool down eventually, don't you think?" Cade's lack of understanding of how girls work rivals mine. But he doesn't let that stop him; he keeps right on with the meeting. We've all got busy days, and we need to make the most of this morning.

"Okay, so you've got the paperwork going. Tell me again what the plan is for the mill. It's the focus now?" Chance scribbles a few notes on the legal pad in front of him. He and Cade have matching dimples in their chins and the same hazel eyes.

"Here's the part where we need your help. Faith has a pretty good idea of how we would use the building once we got it purchased and restored, but we're not close to that yet. I'm not sure how much the restoration would cost, and we're not even sure we'd be able to raise enough money to buy it in the first place." Cade gives me an apologetic look. "Plus we're all busy. This can't take away from our real jobs."

"Look, this whole thing was Molly's idea," I volunteer. "If y'all don't think it's going to work out, then we can let it go." I think about the mill being torn down to build McMansions and I shudder a little. But I would get over that eventually.

"Let's not give up on it so soon." Chance rubs his chin and scribbles a few more notes on the pad. "It fits with our brand, and it would be nice to be able to have a positive impact on preserving some of Mint Springs' history. Not to play down the philanthropic part of this, but it would be good business for us."

"I would think it would be good business for more than just us. Happy Trails would get a boost. We could play that part up to other local businesses. I have a list started of potential donors; I can show that to you." Cade shuffles some papers. "What do you think? We try to move ahead?"

"I'd see if you could entice Molly back to help. We'd need her connections. Can't have all of the Junior Leaguers out for blood." Chance chuckles to himself. He has obviously never been on the losing end of a fight with a Junior Leaguer. "But I think we could still have the festival."

I perk up at this. I do love a party. "We could? But the mill won't be ready. We aren't even sure if they'll let us use it."

"They might not even let us buy it." Cade doesn't make eye contact with me. He's been in talks with the owners, and they have been seeing dollar signs for a while now. It's hard to make them think goodwill beats cold, hard cash, even if they would like the mill to stay standing.

"We can have the festival on our farm. If we make use of the events barn we can also showcase our property. That space is nearly finished, and if you wanted to do something in the fall, the timing would be right." Chance looks from me to Cade. "You could fundraise. Is that too late? Will they have sold the place by then?"

"I think they might hold off if they think we're serious. I'll call them again today. You don't think another event's going to kill us?" Cade's joking, but he and his brothers have plenty on their schedules already.

"It might, but at least this one can be written off as tax deductible. That's provided you get all your paperwork together. It'll be fun. Molly gets her Hallmark movie festival and we get to lure people to the restaurant and distillery. Maybe get a little buzz about events we can host in the big barn. Let me know what we need to do to help." Chance is already standing. "I'll see if I can get my notes together for the mill renovation and maybe get a rough estimate. Once we have a budget, we can see how much we need to raise."

"Sounds good." Cade's organizing his things.

I have been zero help in this meeting.

"Do you need me to do anything? You've ended up doing most of the work here." I feel a little twinge of guilt.

"I do need you to do one thing." Cade leans back in his chair and peers down the hall. "Coast is clear. Come over here."

It's like I'm the fish on the line and Cade's just reeling me in. I'm going over to him despite any misgivings, and I'm not dragging my feet. When I'm close, Cade swivels his chair and pulls me into his lap. He wraps his arms around me and kisses me thoroughly enough to have me forgetting all about the fact that we're ten feet away from Chance's office. The door to the conference room is open, and since this is a family business, there's no telling who else could be wandering the building.

"There. That was what I needed." Cade cups my chin in his hand, running his thumb over my lips. "What's the rest of your day look like?"

"I'm at the farm to look at the rest of the planting schedule. Got to get those fall and winter veggies planned." None of that sounds important anymore. Who needs anything but this right here? I'm in dangerous territory if I'm thinking of Cade instead of how much broccoli to plant, but I can't bring myself to care.

"You think you can find some time tonight?" Cade already knows the answer to that question.

"For you? Of course."

Because I'd move heaven and earth for five more minutes with him.

## 27

*Cade*

I've created a monster. The best kind of monster, mind you, but an insatiable monster all the same. It's like Faith's a volcano that's been lying dormant for years and now is nothing but hot lava going everywhere. Not that I'm complaining, I'm the recipient of this crazy sexual energy and I don't mind it one bit.

I'm waking up in her bed again with the sun peeking through the curtains. Faith's gone, of course, because somehow she's able to burn the candle at both ends. I'd come over under the guise of talking about the mill, but from the second I walked in the door, we were all about getting naked. Faith's house isn't as comfortable as mine, but there's no way I could have her come over to my place without rousing suspicion. Although it's less likely anyone would be suspicious and more likely someone would catch us in the act. I've always loved the unlocked doors and open invitations of living on the farm with my brothers, but right now I'm wishing for a little more privacy.

I stretch my arms over my head. I wouldn't have thought

I'd be sore this morning, but there you go. Faith wants to try *everything,* and sometimes that means twisting ourselves into positions no human should attempt. I'm going to have to remember to take it easy on my run this morning.

The front door creaks open, and my favorite farmer comes bounding into the bedroom two seconds later. I swear she is the cutest thing I've ever seen, even on two hours of sleep. She jumps on the bed, nearly knocking me onto the floor.

"Are you just waking up? I was expecting breakfast." She rises up on her knees and puts her hands on her hips.

"You were? So demanding." I reach out and pull her on top of me, digging my hands into the flesh of her ass. She's surprisingly muscular under all that denim, and I've loved getting to discover all sorts of things about the body I've been dreaming about for years.

"How about I have you for breakfast, then?" They're daring words she never would have used before, but Faith is coming into her own lately.

"Is that a promise or a threat?" I try to flip over and get her on her back, but Faith is having none of it. She resists and raises up until she's straddling me, only the sheet between us covering my naked body.

Faith slides her overall straps down and frees her upper body. Then she pulls her T-shirt over her head and throws it behind her.

"Were you braless under there?" I marvel at Faith's chest. "Full of surprises this morning." I move to sit up and pull one of those tempting nipples into my mouth, but Faith leans back.

"Not so fast." She puts one hand on my chest like she's keeping me down. In reality, I could overpower her if I wanted to and we both know it, but when Faith feels like taking charge, I'm more than happy to let her. "Stay right there. Don't move." She climbs off me, slides out of her overalls, and lets them puddle there next to the bed. Then she climbs right back on.

"Ah, that is better." I move my fingers along the groove of her spine, tracing the bones with my fingers. "Now, about your breakfast."

"Right." Faith wiggles a little, and I know she can already feel my erection between us. Now that she's down to her panties, there's not much left to the imagination, and it doesn't take much to get me ready to go. She leans over and captures my mouth. She already smells of sunshine and soft earth, and I breathe in the lemony smell of her hair as a few tendrils brush my face. I cup her jaw with one hand and try to ease her down over me, but she resists.

"What are you up to?"

"Relax for a second." It's a whisper in my ear right before Faith's tongue slides down the side of my neck.

I close my eyes and try to stay still, but Faith's mouth is moving along my collarbone, softly nipping, making it hard not to be too wiggly. I can feel her smile against my skin as she moves lower, tasting my chest and belly. She slides the sheet lower, kissing along my hip bones, just brushing my cock as she goes from one side to the other.

"That's teasing." I whisper, but I'm not counting on Faith taking that as a challenge.

"It's not teasing; it's the build up." Her smile isn't the sweet one she usually gives me when she raises her eyes to meet mine. Right now, Faith's more devil than angel.

"You don't have to." Faith came into this with less experience than I had realized, but her eagerness more than makes up for all of that. It's something Charlie would probably point out as a good reason to give me a knuckle sandwich, but it's one of the many things he's never going to find out. And no one can say I'm taking advantage. Even if Faith's a more than willing participant now, I still don't want her to do anything she doesn't want to.

"What did you say to me before?" Faith raises her head, looking up the length of my body. "This isn't a have to, it's a want to? This is a want to, Cade."

I take her at her word and let my head fall back on the pillow. "Go on, then."

"Don't forget to talk. I won't get any better without feed-back." Faith is nothing if not a serious student. What she fails to understand is how difficult it can be for me to critique anything at all once my dick's in her mouth.

"Um-hum." It's barely out before the only sound I can make is a gurgle. My hips come up off the bed involuntarily, and I have to fight the urge to keep rocking them.

Faith hums a little and the sensation goes through my entire body. Some women only give blow jobs out of obliga-tion, but Faith doesn't bother pretending to like things she doesn't. She slides her mouth lower and takes me deeper than she has before.

"That's new," I grind out, but I don't really want Faith to stop what she's doing to give me any details about where she learned it.

"New good or new bad?" Faith sounds like she's taking notes.

"Good, so good." I'd say more, but once Faith gets back to work all I want is to get to keep feeling her tongue circling the tip of my cock the way I've told her drives me wild. I groan as Faith's hand starts to slide up and down in tandem with her mouth. This is way better than pancakes.

"Faith," I pant. "I'm getting close. Slide up here."

"Nuh-uh." She doesn't stop what she's doing.

"Faith." It's a plea. If she doesn't stop in the next few seconds we are going to be at the point of no return. "Come on, it's your turn." I give the top of her arms a little yank.

She releases me from her mouth with a *pop*. "Let me do this. Maybe I like it."

I start to protest, but Faith is back to business, and my eyes are already rolling back in their sockets. And it does something to me to have so many of Faith's firsts be with me. I shouldn't want that, especially since I already know I'm too attached. I've broken Charlie's trust, and eventually he'll find that out. I've done things with Faith I can't take back, and the scariest part is I wouldn't want to take them back if I could. So I let her keep going, and when I need to finish, I let Faith keep me where I am even if it means I'm going straight to hell. It feels too good to be with her and even better to give her what she wants.

Faith slides back up my body and rests her head on my chest as I try to catch my breath. "How was that?" She's still sweet, but she just let me come in her mouth and had no problem swallowing it down.

"Perfect," I tell her. There are plenty of other adjectives to describe this morning: dangerous, selfish, X-rated. I'll get her opinion once my heart stops threatening to beat out of my chest. I'm always careful to get a temperature check as we go along. An unhappy Faith isn't ever what I want, and I never want to be the cause of it. "Your turn now."

Faith basically purrs in my ear. "What are you going to do?"

"Wait and see." Because after that I'm going to have a hard time not giving her whatever she wants.

## 28

---

*Faith*

I ring the doorbell and straighten out the hem of my skirt. I've tried to make myself presentable in the hopes that Molly will see that as an olive branch. Showing up in my overalls would have shown less interest in having her accept my apology, but I also wouldn't be fussing with my outfit on the porch when Molly's enormous front door swings open. I've already got on my most remorseful face, ready to beg for forgiveness. I'm here to mend fences so Molly will come back to help us with Cutter's Mill. I'm armed with a plate of the only thing I can bake—oatmeal cookies—and the offer that Molly can technically be the president of the Historical Society as long as Cade and I can be co-presidents. But I'm tempted to make some of that negotiable if that's what it takes, because we could really use some of Molly's manpower.

But it isn't Molly who's standing on the other side of the tall wooden door. I peer down to find myself looking into the big blue eyes of one of Molly's children. He's maybe four or five and he's wearing one of the little shortall outfits

Molly sells through her at home business, Smock It to Me. His little overalls have a fire truck smocked on the front bib. Molly does a fair amount of business around here, especially at Christmas. And though I would never put my own child in something that couldn't end up covered in dirt by the end of the day, I can assure you my sisters will be keeping Molly in business as soon as one of them gets a positive pregnancy test.

"Is your mommy at home?" I try to make myself closer to eye-level.

Molly's son doesn't say anything; he turns around and goes back into the house without even closing the door.

"That's a yes, maybe?" I stand on the threshold. I'm pretty confident my apology will go over better if I don't surprise Molly in the shower. "Molly?" I call out, hoping she can hear me from wherever she is in this giant house.

Obviously she doesn't hear me yelling from here on the porch and so I stand there like an idiot as all of the air conditioning pours out through the open door. Molly's been ignoring my calls and texts, and Cade's too, so even though I'd tried to warn her in advance that I would be stopping by, she doesn't know. Or she does and that's why I'm standing out here in the heat with my plate of rapidly melting apology cookies.

"Faith?" Molly's head eventually peeks around the corner of one of the front rooms. "Why are you standing there with the door open?" She frowns at me, and for once I know I deserve it.

"One of your boys opened it. Firetruck on his little outfit. Cute, by the way." I shuffle the plate of cookies from one hand to the other. "About this tall." I indicate with my free hand, putting out my palm like it makes a difference.

"What are you doing here?" Molly's stance is firm, and

her hands are already on her hips. She's not dressed to go out or for company, really, either.

"Didn't you get my texts? I tried to tell you I was coming over." I try to muster up one of the nice smiles my sisters would use in this kind of a situation. Neutral but welcoming, not too much teeth.

Molly's expression doesn't change. "I blocked your number."

"Blocked?" The nerve. "That's a little extreme, don't you think?"

"No, I do not." Her shiny brown pony tail shakes in indignation. "I would say when someone steals something right out from under you, blocking their number isn't nearly drastic enough."

"I guess you aren't going to invite me in?" I try to make it sound hopeful, like it might be a possibility.

"Why would I do that?"

"Because I brought cookies?" I hold out the plate, the little discs arranged in the fan pattern my mother taught me.

"You made those?" Molly's wrinkling up her nose, but it's making her come closer. "I didn't think you could bake."

"I can only make these. I'm not good in the kitchen the way you are." Ah, the flattery. I'm hoping that helps my cause. "There are plenty of things you're good at that I can't possibly do. That's why I'm here to apologize."

Molly cocks her head to one side. "Apologize?"

"Yes, and to ask you to please come back to the Historical Society. We really need you. I'm so sorry if Cade and I made it seem like we didn't want your input." I'd practiced this part a few times with my mother and then again with Cade. The words don't roll off my tongue, but they don't stick in my craw the way they did yesterday.

"You two were pretty rude." Molly waits for me to acknowledge that. She isn't going to make this easy.

I take a big breath. I don't think we were rude, but if that's what it takes... "You're right. We could have been more thoughtful in our presentation."

Molly huffs. "And it was my idea in the first place. It was unfair for you and Cade to swoop in and try to kick me out."

"We never wanted to kick you out, Molly. We wanted a few changes, that's all."

"Changes like me not being the founder. That was a bitter pill to swallow after *I* invited *you* to join. Without me there wouldn't even be a Historical Society. You two wouldn't even know about the mill." She waits for me to give her credit.

"You're right about that, too, and it turns out we need the things you bring to the table. And I don't want to ruin our friendship, Molly. Cade is just sick that you and I can't be friends over this." That's a lie I hope is a little white one. Molly Eagan might not be the first person I would think of when I name people in my circle of friends, but she was kind enough to let me be in her group. She was generous with her time, and other than her inherent bossiness, her heart's in the right place.

"Really?"

"Most definitely."

"Aw." Molly's rushes to the door and her arms encircle me. "I missed you, too. You'll have to tell Cade we made up. But I'm not sure about the Historical Society. My feelings were really hurt." She gives me a sad look. "I don't know how I can come back if I'm not the president."

Tricky, tricky woman.

"Well, we were talking, and Cade and I were thinking we could all be co-presidents."

Molly's arms go right back to her sides. "Co-presidents?" She makes it sound like I've offered her the opportunity to clean my toilet.

"Yes, but you would be the founder. No argument there." I hold my breath.

"I'm not sure I'm interested in that." Molly reaches for the plate and takes the cookies out of my hand. "Thank you for the cookies, though. I'm sure the kids will enjoy them." Her hand reaches for the door, and I get the feeling I'm about to have it slammed in my face.

"But we need you for the festival." I lean my head around the edge of the rapidly closing door. "Did I mention we might have figured out a way to have your fall festival?"

Molly's front door opens back up. "You did? Why didn't you tell me that in the first place? Come in, come in! We have to get started on that right away. Summer will be over before you know it!"

And I slide into the front hallway before she can change her mind.

## 29

*Cade*

There's nothing that can jolt me from the high I'm on right now. I'm running a little late getting back from Faith's this morning, but skipping my run doesn't feel like a sacrifice at all after the last few hours. I'm tired but energized at the same time. Pretty much ready to take on just about anything.

Until I see Chance walking up the road toward me.

He startles a bit once I get closer, and there's no way I can't stop and roll down the car window to chat even though my first instinct is to push my foot hard on the gas pedal and speed right on by. It's not like I can sink low enough in my seat for him not to know it's me.

"Hey, where've you been? We were looking for you." Chance leans down until his face is nearly even with mine.

"Out driving." Common sense tells me I should have anticipated a moment like this and come up with a better story, but I'm not skilled at lying and right now it shows.

Chance's eyebrows lift a little and his mouth thins, but

he doesn't come right out and accuse me of fibbing. "In your clothes from yesterday?"

"Oh." I look down at the rumpled shirt. It still smells lightly of Faith's skin. She'd been wearing it while we ate breakfast and taking it back off of her had delayed me even further. I fight the smile the memory triggers and shrug. "I guess." *Idiot.*

Chance lets my non-answer slide. "We've got a little situation with the grand opening."

"What do you mean?" That falls squarely in the red alert category. The grand opening for the restaurant is in a few days, and it needs to go off without a hitch. Charlie and Jenna have been working their butts off to get the menu right and train all the new staff members. I cross my fingers that it isn't a mistake I've made. I'm usually pretty meticulous in all the work stuff, but I've been distracted lately. It wouldn't be like me from a few weeks ago to make a mistake, but current me would probably be ripe for that kind of thing. In fact, I should take some time today to double-and triple-check the things I've approved recently.

"Mom and Dad were both invited and they've both RSVP'd yes."

"How did that happen?" At least I wasn't in charge of the guest list. That's not a mistake I would have made, though. If there was a snowball's chance in hell our parents would end up in the same room at the same time, I'd have canceled the whole event.

"We'll talk about it in a bit. You best get on home and shower so no one asks who she is. You smell one hundred percent like one-night stand." Chance smirks.

Part of me wants to tell Chance he's wrong, to brag that Faith is more than a one-time thing. But Faith is supposed to be a never thing, an absolutely-don't-mess-with-her thing, and spilling the fact that I've been sleeping at her house so much I can't remember what the inside of my own bedroom looks like is not going to win me any friends. And what would I tell him, anyway? Faith and I haven't had that conversation. So I let him think whatever he wants, and luckily, he doesn't ask for a name. Again, I'm not great with lies, and having to make up some woman from the Niagara Falls area would give me away for sure. This town isn't exactly full of tourists, and I wouldn't want to pretend to have something going with a local who knows nothing about my deception.

"Can you do me a favor and not mention this to everyone else?" It's the kind of thing Chance would normally tell Cooper and Charlie so they could bust my chops, but more scrutiny will expose my weak alibi for sure.

"Maybe," Chance teases. "But you'll owe me one." He's only half-joking.

"I'd appreciate it."

"Man's gotta do what a man's gotta do." Chance moves away from the window to let me get home. "Just be careful."

I think about asking him what he means by that, but decide I don't really want to know. I don't need any brotherly advice about how I've already crossed the line.

*You have got to be kidding me.*

I slam the front door and stomp into my house. Of course our family meeting about the invitation slip-up would end with me on the hook. After realizing there's nothing to do but suck it up and try to keep our parents from killing each other, every head had turned to look at me. Of course I'll try to entertain Mom while everyone else does their thing at the opening. Charlie's busy with the restaurant, Cooper will be busy with the distillery, and Chance isn't close enough to our mother to do the job.

So it falls to me to spend the entire evening babysitting instead of putting out the million other fires I'm going to just trust someone else will take care of. I take a deep breath. I hadn't said much about the unfairness of this assignment in our meeting. How could I really have argued that someone else should do it? We weren't going to unin-vite anyone, and that means dealing with things as they are —Jeff Allen and Abigail Allen ready to throw bombs at one another at a moment's notice, or, less likely, behaving like civilized adults at a social function. We'll see, I guess.

I change into my running clothes. Office time can wait a bit longer. Right now I need to work off some of this aggres-sion before I see any of my family members. I lace my shoes up tight and don't even bother to stretch. I'm on the gravel road in two seconds, letting the heat of the morning focus all my energy on putting one foot in front of the other.

And it is already hot. This sticky Georgia heat is exactly why I prefer to run before the sun's had much time in the sky. Some days the humidity makes it feel like you're swim-ming through soup, and I don't need that. Today isn't horri-ble, but I'm already sweating before I take my detour off the main road and down the path through the trees. It's cooler here, and I fill my lungs with the pine-scented air. I let the rhythm of my footsteps and the crunch of needles under my shoes soothe the churning of my stomach and the pounding of my head. It's my usual loop. It takes me along the edge of the property, but keeps me in the tree line. During hunting season I have to make sure to wear my safety orange, but I prefer the tiny hills and valleys of this route to the one I could take on the road. There's less of a possibility of one of my siblings accidentally showing up and wanting me to stop and talk and even less of a possibility of anyone wanting to come with me. Some mornings there's mist rising off the pond, and usually the only sound other than my own breathing and footsteps is the chirping of birds and the occasional cricket. The forest sounds are better than anything I could pipe through my headphones, and by the time I wrap my way back around the edge of the farm, I'm feeling slightly more in control. I weave my way back toward my aunts' house and their garden hose, ready to spray myself down with cold water and take a surreptitious drink. Even though we drank from the hose all the time as kids, as an adult I'm supposed to plan ahead and bring a container that doesn't have all kinds of junk growing in it. As an adult I'm supposed to know better.

"Cade Allen, you had better not be drinking out of that hose."

I jump and pull the green plastic tubing away from my mouth. Busted.

Sadie comes down the front steps already shaking a finger at me. "You know better than to drink out of that nasty thing. You'll get cholera or something."

I reach for the spigot to turn the water off. "I don't think I'll get cholera, Sadie, and it hasn't killed me yet."

"If I had a nickel for every time one of you told me that... Just because something hasn't killed you yet isn't an excuse to keep doing it." The chickens gather at our feet, picking a little at our shoes. "Did you run in this heat? Come inside and get a real glass of water." Sadie wipes her forehead of imaginary sweat. Her house is air-conditioned now so I know she isn't burning up from two minutes outside. There was a time when both her house and my grandfather's only had fans to move the air around. That made for plenty of late-night fights as my brothers and I tried to negotiate the best breeze.

"I'm fine. I need to run back home and get ready for work. The hose water already did the trick." I smile at my aunt even though I know she's going to scowl.

"You have plans with Faith today?" It's an innocent question, but Sadie's expression changes as she waits for my answer. I'm not sure what that's about, but it makes me extra careful with my words.

"Not today."

"Well, that's a shame. After that meeting we had earlier, it might be nice to get to visit with her, don't you think? She's always a little ray of sunshine."

Five minutes with Faith would improve my mood considerably, but I can't tell that to Sadie, so I only shrug. "I assume she's got a busy day today."

"Don't let that opportunity pass you by, Cade." Sadie gives me a wink. "I'm going back inside before I melt." And she leaves me standing there in the yard before I can ask her what she means.

## 30

*Faith*

I'm loading the last crate for this morning's deliveries when my mother comes walking down the hill. It's early, and even if my mother still gets up to make my father's breakfast, she usually isn't down here near the barn or the vegetables before noon.

"Daddy's not here," I yell, hoping to give her enough time to turn around before she wastes any more steps. "He's out on the tractor turning that back field." We rotate the crops on a schedule, and between now and next month we'll start getting things ready for the winter vegetables. It's a constant dance between harvest and preparation that goes all year long.

"I didn't come out here to see your daddy; I came out here to see you." My mother hands me something wrapped in wax paper. "I made you one of those egg sandwiches you like."

I can't exactly tell my mother I've already been served scrambled eggs this morning, especially since explaining that would mean explaining how I got breakfast in bed from a man who isn't supposed to be anywhere near my bedroom. I tuck the sandwich into the front pocket of my overalls. "I'll eat this on the road. Thank you."

"You seem busier than normal lately." It's an invitation to talk, the kind my mother doesn't extend unless she thinks there's something to say.

"The Historical Society is taking up a chunk of time, I guess, and getting all these deliveries out every morning is a big task. Did Daddy tell you we're thinking about hiring a driver? We've got enough clients now to make that happen." It's something I'm extremely proud of since the small-batch deliveries were my idea. Clients are asking for bigger orders, and I can't handle it all myself. It's a good problem to have, one that means expanding the business at a time when we thought it might not be possible.

"You'd give up the deliveries? I thought you liked getting out and seeing people." Mama rests her hand on the side of my truck, and I can see she's not going to let me go without more of a chat.

"I might keep some of them. I do like checking in at Ham & Eggs and the local places. It helps me anticipate what they might order next." I shuffle my feet a little and give the last crate a shove. Normally I'd be closing the tailgate and getting moving. I don't like to waste time, and now that I've got the Allens as my last delivery, I hope to see Cade for a second or two before I have to be back home.

"You'd keep Charlie's delivery, I assume."

"Probably, unless it gets too big for my truck. I've got the gardens over there too so I can't really give the Allens to a delivery guy." And I wouldn't want to because it would mean giving up all the stolen moments I have with Cade. We're reckless now around his farm, and even though we both keep saying we can't keep taking those chances, we both keep doing it.

"Then you'd better get going, I suppose." Mama's mouth doesn't curl up into a smile. I'm not sure what she came out here to accomplish, but she doesn't seem all that pleased. "Don't want to keep people waiting."

"No, ma'am." I shut the tailgate but my mother doesn't start the walk back to the house.

"Just remember to be good, Faith."

"I will, Mama." I suddenly feel like a five-year-old again. "I always am."

"I was going to get to that."

I don't even bother lifting my head to look at Charlie. "No, you weren't." I grab another clump of grass and give it a tug.

"I've been doing it when I can. Give me two seconds and I'll come and help you." Charlie's dressed to work in the kitchen, not to weed garden beds.

"This is part of my job, Charlie, and you're busy with the rest of yours. I'm not here to make you feel guilty; I'm here to make sure this bed isn't overrun with dandelions." But feeling guilty seems to be the main thing I do these days when Charlie's involved. He must be feeling the same way, because even though I've given him permission to leave, he stays put.

"If you can leave it until later, we can work on it together."

"It'll be too hot. I'll leave a few for you to pull when you get the chance, how about that?" I fight the urge to roll my eyes. "Don't you have a grand opening to get ready for?"

Charlie lets out a big breath. "Yes."

"Then go do what you need to do. I can't have the beds I put in looking unkempt for your party but it isn't your job to help me make that happen. It is your job to go and run that restaurant, so get your butt back in there." I wave Charlie toward the backdoor. "Go on."

"Once things calm down a little, we should make some plans."

I can't help but make a face. Charlie and I don't schedule things—we've never needed to. Even when he'd be dating some girl from town, he and I would still find time to do things together. "Things aren't going to calm down, Charlie, and we both know why."

His face wrinkles up, but he can't deny it. "It'll get easier once the restaurant is up and running."

"Charlie, we haven't gone fishing all summer. Not once have you come by Happy Trails. I'd be willing to bet you haven't even been in the river except for that float trip. The restaurant's part of that, but we both know where you want to spend your time and with *whom*. It's fine." I rip another weed from the ground. "I'm busy too."

That gets Charlie's attention. "With work or with something else?"

"What does it matter?" I shoot him a warning glance. Charlie doesn't get to be obsessed with his voluptuous chef and then give me grief about how I spend my time.

"You seem to have plenty of time for Cade." Normally there'd be a little teasing there, but Charlie's not even cracking a smile. And the worst part is that what he's insinuating is true. I do have plenty of time for his brother, in ways he probably would regret knowing about if I told him.

I stand and pull my gloves from my hands. "We're working on a project together. It was your suggestion to have him help me." Even as I'm saying it I know it isn't fair to try to make Charlie feel guilty. I'm using his own words to cover up the reality of what Cade and I are doing.

"Sorry." His apology puts a dagger in my heart. I might be sad that my friendship with Charlie is changing, but I'm the one who's really hiding things. Eventually the truth always comes out. In a town as small as Mint Springs, someone's bound to talk. Charlie will be furious when it happens, but it's too late now, and I'm making it worse because I'm covering the lie with my indignation. My outsized reaction isn't because I can't believe Charlie would think there's something between Cade and I, it's because there is.

"Go back to work and let me finish up here. I'll come inside and steal some coffee from you when I'm done, okay?" I try to soften things, and it works. Charlie reaches out and musses the top of my head before he goes back inside the restaurant.

It's only when I turn around that I see Cade. I'm not sure how long he's been standing there or how much he heard but it doesn't matter. My heart speeds up in my chest. All the guilty feelings in the world won't make me want him less. Nothing Charlie says or does now will make those feelings go away. When Cade walks up and kisses me long and hard —in plain view of anyone who bothers to walk back here—I don't even consider pulling away.

## 31

*Cade*

The party is going as well as can be expected. There are a few hiccups here and there, but nothing that derails anything we've planned. My brothers all look sharp in their suits, and the guest list for the grand opening is full of heavy hitters. Jenna's food is on point, and all the buildings look fabulous. None of that's my responsibility, of course. I know to stay in my lane. I wouldn't dream of telling Charlie or Jenna how to run the kitchen. I might think there's too much pepper in the grit cakes they're serving or wish we'd gone with the pecan pie for dessert, but I keep my mouth shut.

The same thing goes for Cooper's liquor. He's the master distiller; I'm merely an amateur. I've got opinions, but unless there's a huge mistake being made, I keep those to myself. Do I prefer a spicier rye whiskey to a smoky one? Damn straight I do. But that doesn't mean I need to boss my brother about it. It isn't my area of expertise.

I can't tell tulle from cotton, truth be told, so I keep my nose out of Lily's business. I don't dare tell Chance his decision to use the old barn wood for the distillery floor isn't what I would have wanted. It turned out great, the mix of the old and the new are perfect, even if I couldn't see that at first. The color of the walls and the arrangement of the tables isn't anything I'd ever question. When it comes to all that, they're the professionals.

So you'd think when it comes to corralling our mother and keeping her away from our father, they'd all let me do my thing. I know more about keeping Abigail Allen in check than all of them combined. But that's not how it goes. Cooper would never second-guess my profit projections. Chance would never ask me if I was sure when I tell him anything about the bank balance. Charlie wouldn't think twice about my advice when it comes to budgeting for his food costs. They'd all trust I knew what I was doing. But when it comes to our mother, they've all got advice and opinions they just cannot keep to themselves.

"If you needed to, you could take her to see the houses. She'd like that, I bet." Chance's great idea would mean our mother and father were as far apart as possible, but would also mean I'd be driving her around the farm like it was some kind of parade of homes. We've all got houses out here now, and tours of all of them would mean missing the entire event.

"You could try to keep her up at the distillery until the last second. Sneak her in to the restaurant right before dinner starts." Cooper's suggestion isn't the worst, but it all but ensures I'll be sneaking in right before dinner starts too. Again, not how I had envisioned participating in this event.

"I'd be sure to keep her out of the kitchen. There are knives in there." Charlie's oh-so-helpful addition was the last straw.

"Why are y'all so concerned with making sure Mom

doesn't do anything? What, Jeff Allen's going to be on his best behavior? Which one of you's going to be making sure he doesn't start something?"

No one had answered me, of course, and so I'd trudged along, basically holding Mom's hand while our father traipsed around like a king. He was infuriating to watch, all right, but no one went for any knives.

"Do you need another drink, Mama?" I was trying to be hospitable without loading her up on the alcohol.

"Oh, no. I'm fine." She gives me one of her arm pats. "Would you look at that? I don't remember Faith having all those sisters."

I look across the room to where Faith's sitting with her family.

"Four girls, can you imagine?" My mother makes a little clucking noise. "That house must have been interesting when they were growing up."

"People probably said the same thing about our house. Four boys has to be wilder than four girls." I laugh a little and my mother does too.

"That's true. Never a dull moment with four sons." She looks back across the room and whispers, "They all turned out so pretty."

I risk another look at Faith. Her sisters are dressed to the nines, but I wouldn't have expected anything less. They do look pretty, their hair done up and their faces in full paint. But none of them outshines Faith. She catches me staring and gives me the tiniest smile before she averts her eyes. It's like I can breathe for the first time all night, and I smile back even though she doesn't see it.

"Oh. Well." My mother's looking at me like she's just put the last piece of a puzzle together. So much for keeping my feelings to myself. "Cade Allen, I would not have guessed that."

I try to play it off like it's nothing. "We're working on a project together."

"I'll bet you are." Her smile's the kind that hints at mischief, and even though it's at my expense, I try to appreciate it. I don't get many conspiratorial smiles from my mother these days. "You aren't going to go talk to her? Say hello to her daddy?"

"Not tonight."

That disappoints her, but she doesn't push, and I'm grateful for that. Maybe later I'll get five minutes with Faith, but for now I'm where I'm supposed to be, even if I'd love to be across the room holding Faith's hand instead of making sure my icy glare keeps my father from coming anywhere near my mother.

It goes faster than I anticipate, and before long Charlie's calling me to the front of the room with the rest of my brothers. There's champagne for a toast, and my brothers all say a few words. I'm in the background like always, but it isn't like I'm itching to give a speech. Charlie and Cooper thank their wives, and I make myself look as far away from Faith as possible. What would that feel like, to be able to be open and honest in front of everyone? My father's smiling face catches my eye, and he raises his glass at me. Any warm feelings I might have been nurturing fade as quickly as they came.

When it's Charlie's turn to speak, I don't begrudge him the spotlight. He's worked hard to get us where we are tonight. We've finally decided on a name for the restaurant, and it's up to him to make the announcement. Of course he showers Jenna with praise, but I try not to let that bother me. She's been working hard, too, and Charlie's promised us all he's keeping things all business.

"And another one of Jenna's brilliant ideas has to do with the name of this restaurant." Charlie looks at Jenna, and she smiles back at him. "We've gone back and forth about what we should call this place. We all agreed we wanted something that really showed you not only the kind of food you would get here, but the way you would be treated. We wanted you to get a taste of what it was like for the four of us coming here every summer and being made to feel like the most cherished kids in the world. Our grandfather isn't here tonight, but Cooper's first whiskey is named after him. We're hoping to have that ready for tasting next year. Some of y'all are already drinking Sadie's gin and Hadley's moonshine. Mae's apple brandy's hitting the shelves in a few weeks. My brothers and I have made a commitment to being part of this community and to honoring our family. That's why we've decided to name this restaurant after the two ladies who really taught us about food and family and farm. Welcome to Sadie Mae's, y'all. The sign goes up tomorrow."

There's a round of thunderous applause as Sadie and Mae react to the news. We'd meant it as a surprise, and they don't seem to have suspected anything. I'm so focused on my aunts and the hoopla around them, you'd think I might be able to avoid Charlie's next big surprise. He makes that impossible, of course, as he leans over and kisses Jenna in a way no one is going to describe as business-like. Cooper, Chance, and I can't do anything but stare as Charlie plunders the mouth of our executive chef.

## 32

*Faith*

Charlie sure knows how to stop a show, that's for sure. One minute we're all celebrating the new name of the restaurant, lifting our glasses to toast Sadie and Mae, and the next we're all picking our jaws up off the floor after Charlie planted one on Jenna in front of everyone. None of Charlie's brothers look happy about that maneuver, even though Charlie looks like the cat who ate the canary. I half expect him to start pulling yellow feathers out of his mouth.

"Oh, my goodness." My mother isn't the only one having that reaction. There are a few gasps and some whispered comments.

Cooper, Chance, and Cade are stuck standing in front of us all, eyes popping out of their sockets as Charlie and Jenna do their tongue tangle. Luckily, Chance has the good sense to bring everyone's attention back to the restaurant and its new name. He herds the other brothers over to Sadie and Mae's table, where they make a big show of hugging. I'm not sure what Charlie was thinking, but he's taken away from a moment that should have been about his entire family and made it about himself.

Cade eventually stomps off, and Cooper takes his seat at the table next to their mother. I guess Cade's finally been given a five-minute break from his job of keeping their parents apart. I don't know everything about the divorce their parents went through, but I know it was messy. Still, you'd think two grown people would be able to handle themselves for one evening. I itch to chase after Cade, but running out of here will only attract attention, and I've already seen what that looks like tonight. No, thanks. I wait until I can't stand it anymore and excuse myself.

"Where are you off to?" Charity gives me a little smirk. She's wearing a red dress that's a show-stopper in and of itself. All my sisters are dolled up within an inch of their lives and squeezed into tight-fitting cocktail dresses. There aren't many occasions in Mint Springs where you can dress to impress, and they have taken advantage of the opportunity. Hope, Charity, and Constance Baker are dazzling.

Me? Meh. I tried. I don't have a closet full of dresses, and I refused to let anyone take me on a "helpful" shopping trip. I am wearing lipstick, and the dress I have on isn't a garbage bag so I feel presentable. I smooth the front of the blue fabric again as I try to make my escape.

"I need to run to the ladies room." It's not exactly a lie because I fully intend to walk right past it on my way to scour the parking lot for Cade.

"Your sister is allowed to mingle," Mama tells the table tartly. For some reason she's exceptionally easy to deal with tonight. I doubt she really thinks I'm going to the bathroom, but she won't want a discussion of it either way.

"Thank you, Mama." I nearly stick my tongue out at Charity.

"You'd better tell us everything you find out," Connie threatens. Of course they think I'm off to question Charlie about his lip lock. I ignore her and make my way to the back of the restaurant.

It takes longer than I'd planned because there's all the required stops and starts as I move between the tables. Everyone who is anyone is here, and that means saying hello and asking after babies and grandmas over and over again. Then I am well and truly standing outside the bathroom door, and I still haven't caught even a glimpse of Cade.

"Hey, come here." It's a low rumble in my ear accompanied by a tug of my hand. Cade pulls me through the kitchen and out the back door into the thick night air. "I just need five minutes with you."

I'm more than happy to give it. I wrap my arms around his neck and get right to kissing him. As usual, it doesn't take long for us to go from zero to sixty. We've got our hands all over each other when the door from the kitchen swings open, bathing us in light. We break apart, but not nearly soon enough if Jenna's raised eyebrows are any indication.

"Just getting a little air," she says, like she catches Cade and I sneaking around every day of the week. "This isn't the best location for that, but I'm sure you know that already."

I think about begging her to keep what she's seen to herself. I'm positive she's about to run straight to Charlie with every little detail, and I cannot have that. But I don't get to even say a peep because Cade is already pulling me down the road toward the darkened windows of their office building. Wordlessly he pulls his keys from his pocket and unlocks the front door, leads me inside, and shuts it behind us.

"I'll need to get back soon." I say it more for myself than for Cade. He's not the one who'll have trouble leaving. I'd stay here all night in this dark hallway if it meant I got to keep touching him. Again we're hands and mouths and nothing but need.

"We should go in my office."

I'd follow him anywhere, and so I walk behind him, my fingers still intertwined with his. Once we get to the room he uses for work, he shuts the door and clicks the bolt in place.

"You look so pretty." Cade runs his thumbs over my cheekbones, cradling my face in his hands.

"You don't look so bad yourself." I slide my hands over the lapels of his suit jacket, feeling the muscles underneath. He leans into my touch, and I let him kiss me again.

"I was going crazy not being able to touch you." He slides a hand lower, bunching up my skirt to get to skin. My thigh heats under his palm.

I know I should control myself, but the semi-privacy afforded by the locked door makes me forget all the reasons we would keep things PG. I slide Cade's jacket off his shoulders and deposit it on his desk chair.

"I wish we didn't have to stay for the rest of this. I want to be inside you, Faith." Cade's words make me burn and his hand, now firmly between my thighs, isn't helping me make great choices.

"You can. We can be quick." I've long since quit worrying about where my family might think I've gone or what they might think I'm doing. Nothing matters right now but getting as close to Cade as possible.

He eases me onto the surface of his desk, sliding my skirt up as he goes. I fumble with his belt and the button on his suit pants. I'd love to be able to take my time getting him out of this outfit. Cade really does look like a character out of a James Bond movie. His body in a suit fairly screams sex, and I think almost anyone would understand why I'm having trouble listening to the good girl part of me that knows we're taking an even bigger risk than ever before.

"Shit, hold on." Cade fishes around in his pants pocket for his wallet and pulls out a foil packet. "Can't forget this."

In reality we probably could, but Cade and I haven't had that conversation. We can talk about almost anything, but our relationship status isn't up for discussion. What is there to talk about when we're stuck sneaking around?

I help him slide the condom on, and Cade groans against my neck. My legs are already shaking with anticipation when he pulls my panties aside. The rush of cold air against my exposed skin makes me shiver. Cade takes one of his long fingers and drags it through the wetness there. I moan loud enough for them to hear me back at the restaurant.

"You're ready, aren't you, baby?" Cade's mouth touches my ear.

I'm close to begging when he finally goes ahead and gives me what I want, sliding inside me in one slow thrust. Another wall-shaking groan escapes my lips. Half-dressed on Cade's desk in the middle of their grand opening, and I'm about to come apart. Cade keeps up the slow, tortuous rhythm until I can't take it anymore. I claw at his back and writhe against him. The virginal good girl that was Faith Baker is obviously not the woman in this room right now. Nope, you can kiss that girl goodbye.

"Faster. I need faster, Cade."

He gives me what I want, the legs of the desk scraping a little on the floor with each thrust until I can't hold back any more. I throw my head back and let wave after wave of pleasure roll over me. Even my fingers are tingling as Cade kisses my neck and then goes stiff against me. A few seconds later he's smiling against my skin, saying my name like it's the most beautiful word in the entire universe.

As we separate and try to pull ourselves together, we keep sneaking kisses, keep reaching out to touch each other one more time. I straighten Cade's tie and he tries to smooth some of the wrinkles out of the back of my dress.

"I think that might be a lost cause. Do I at least look like maybe I went for a tractor ride or something? People might believe that." I look for my left shoe under the desk. I must have kicked it off at some point.

"Instead of the ride you really took?" Cade seems in much better spirits now than he did twenty minutes ago. He winks at me. "Let's get back to this party. The sooner I get rid of these people and get this place cleaned up, the sooner I can come over to your place and do that again."

We're both laughing as we spill back out into the hall. Cade pulls me in for one more kiss, pressing me against the wall, his hands threading into my hair.

We break apart at the sound of someone clearing their throat behind us.

Cooper. Caught again.

## 33

*Cade*

"You feel like going down to the pond this afternoon?"

I eye my oldest brother suspiciously. "What for?"

"To fish, maybe? I could use a little break." It doesn't seem like a trap, but I'm pretty sure it has to be. Cooper hasn't said a word about finding me and Faith in a compromising position at the grand opening, but eventually he'll have to.

"It's the middle of the work day." I've got my desk covered in the receipts from the grand opening. It isn't like we don't have work to do. I have been a little distracted, though, with thoughts of Faith's bare ass propped on the edge of my work surface. Maybe a little time outside would do me good. "What the hell, sure. Let me run to my house and grab my rod and tackle box."

Cooper's face breaks into a wide grin. "I'll meet you down there in fifteen."

Cooper must run the whole way home and all the way to the pond because when I get there fifteen minutes later, he's already got his line in the water. He's also got a cooler full of beer and two camp chairs, which makes me think this wasn't a spur of the moment invitation. He motions for me to come closer and pats the chair next to his. Now I am smelling a trap.

"We won't catch anything if we sit that close together."

"Who cares if we catch anything?" Cooper asks, rolling his eyes and handing me a beer. "Since when has fishing been about catching fish?"

"Since it was invented. I'll move over to the other side." I start to grab my chair, but Cooper's hand darts out and holds it firm.

"This seat stays here, and your ass needs to go in it." Cooper's pulling out the older brother moves, and there's no arguing with him.

"If you say so." I sit and start to bait my hook. "You want one of these? I had live bait in the fridge."

"From when?"

"A while ago." I can't exactly tell him Faith and I went fishing last week. It took some finagling, but we managed to sneak away for an entire afternoon. For her, fishing is absolutely about catching fish. There's not even kissing until the rods are put away, so I had to make sure to get all my sugar before and after the time at the lake.

"Huh." Cooper seems fine to leave it at that for now. "Secret life of Cade. Seem to be plenty of things I don't know lately."

"I'm sure you don't tell me every tiny detail about your life." I put on of the wiggling worms on the end of my hook, piercing its body through and through.

"I think Faith Baker's more than just a tiny detail." Cooper looks at me from under the brim of his baseball cap. "Pretty sure Charlie'd agree."

"Charlie's an ass." He'd more than proved that when we

confronted him about his stunt at the opening. Basically told us all he knew what he was doing and to mind our own business, like his screwing the executive chef didn't fall into the messiest kind of our business.

"That's undeniably true, but I think he'd have a thing or two to say about you and Faith together. Some of it might even be justified." He pulls back a little on his rod, making the line move a bit in the water. "I'm pretty sure he's told you he doesn't want you messing with her."

Cooper's words irritate me, and I don't do a good job of holding that in. "She's a grown woman; she can decide for herself what she wants. Charlie can go fuck himself." I jerk a little too hard on my fishing rod and have to reel the line all the way in and cast again.

Cooper sits there for a while saying nothing, but I'm sure he's thinking. His silence starts to drive me crazy after a while. If there's one thing I don't need from my brother right now, it's judgment.

"You think I'm taking advantage of her or something? You think I'm making a mistake?" I dare him to ignore me.

"Do you think you are?"

I groan. "I don't need some kind of reverse psychology, Cooper. Charlie told me not to start anything with her, and I did it anyway. Everyone told you to leave Hadley alone and you didn't listen. How's this any different?"

"Well, for starters, 'everyone' didn't include any of my brothers. And I married Hadley. I'm lucky enough to get to start raising babies with her in a few months. That shit's for real. What's this thing you have with Faith?"

I look out over the surface of the pond and avoid Cooper's question.

"And Charlie is going to lose his mind when he finds out, especially if you're just screwing around."

"I'm not screwing around, I..." I'm not sure how to explain to Cooper that happily ever after isn't in the cards for me. Hell, I doubt it's in the cards for anyone. It's nice Cooper and Chance think it's a possibility, but the odds are they'll end up in the same place as our parents. "I'm not sure I'll ever be able to do something long term."

Cooper's face clouds. "You're the most dependable and reliable one out of all of us. It doesn't make any sense to me that you'd think that."

"Statistically, it isn't a great bet." There. Cooper can't argue with those facts.

And he doesn't. Instead he tilts his head back and laughs and laughs. "You think facts have anything to do with this? Oh, Cade. It doesn't work like that. Are you telling me you don't have any feelings for Faith? This is all physical?"

I scowl. "You're scaring away all the fish."

"You're avoiding the question."

"You know I have feelings for her. How can I not? She's perfect." I think about the way Faith runs her business and the way she whispers to me in bed. I think about how fearlessly she asks for what she wants now and how she's the first person I think of in the morning and the person I dream of at night. Imagining her with someone else makes me crazy, but I can't guarantee that's not what's going to happen.

"She's perfect, is she?" Cooper's eyebrows rise under the brim of his cap.

"Well, I know you're probably partial to Hadley, but I think Faith's about as close to perfect as it gets." I reel my line back in and get ready to cast it out again.

"You ever told her that?" Cooper stares out at the water.

"I have, but I'm not sure she believes it." And I don't know if that's going to make a difference when it comes to the way relationships work. I'm walking on a tightrope here, trying to manage my fear and the way I'm drawn to Faith.

"If that's the case, then you'd better call her right now so you can tell her again. Hell, see if she can come out here. I'll give her my chair."

"Are you serious? Charlie'll see."

"I doubt it, and so what if he does? If you think Faith's all that then you shouldn't have to hide her. Let those feelings have a little sunshine. That's the only way to test them." Cooper flicks his line back out into the water. "Hurry up, there's only so much daylight."

I pull out my phone and dial Faith's number. Before I know it she's walking across the pasture toward us, holding her rod. When she gets close enough I kiss her, even though my brother's standing right there. Faith startles but doesn't run, and once she sees Cooper's okay with it, she gives me another. True to his word, Cooper makes himself scarce, but he leaves us the cooler full of beer.

We fish for the next hour or so, not caring who can see us. It feels good to be standing in the sunshine.

## 34

*Faith*

There is not enough aspirin in the world to combat the kind of headache Molly Eagan's friends can give you. We've gone from having no one show up to our Historical Society meetings to packing the conference room at Allen Brothers. When you tell a bunch of small-town ladies there's a party to plan it garners more interest somehow. Now I'm trapped with all the girls I avoided in school talking about bunting and dunking booths and candy apples. And that's got my head pounding.

"It's a *festival*, Faith. We need to keep the messaging clear."

Thank you, Amber Collins for making that point. If it wasn't bad enough to have been bossed around by these girls in middle school, having them do it now was a little extra added bonus. Although today, I didn't actually have to take it. That's right, Faith Baker was still a nice girl when it counted, but she didn't let other people push her around. Not anymore.

"Yes, Amber. I'm well aware it's a *festival*. I'm in charge of it." Maybe that came out a little bitchy, but it made Amber sit up a little straighter for sure.

"Ladies, let's try to stay focused." Molly gives me a warning look. "We have plenty to do and not much time to do it in."

That's the understatement of the year. Planning this festival is more complicated than organizing for next year's crops, and that's a major undertaking. I had thought it would mean hours of logistics, but it turns out it takes hours of *feelings*. There are plenty of feelings on this planning committee. Feelings and thoughts, not to mention suggestions. It's a dance I'm not used to and I keep stepping on people's toes because the feelings and thoughts and suggestions all have to be considered no matter how ridiculous.

I'm trying to leave all that up to Molly.

"The clown idea. Can we get back to that? We have some strong opinions on both sides there."

Cade's managed to miss most of this meeting, lucky duck. But when he finally comes into the conference room, I'm not sure if he's going to be an asset or a distraction. He slides into the chair next to mine and gives my hand a squeeze. No one misses that, apparently, and several eyebrows shoot high into hairlines.

"What did I miss?" He leans close enough to tickle my ear.

"Absolutely nothing. We're currently arguing the merits of clowns versus no clowns." I try to keep my face serious as Cade makes his look like he just ate a lemon.

"Now that Cade's here maybe we should table this discussion and use this time to get some specifics on the venue." Molly turns to look at Cade, giving everyone else an excuse to do the same. "And thank you again for letting us use this room for our meeting. I had no idea y'all had built all this back here." Molly's sugary sweet but I don't think it's all an act. She might have to turn it up a notch with these ladies, but I don't doubt she's sincere.

"Yes," Amber chimes in. "So nice of you and your brothers to let us use this space *and* to donate the use of the space for the festival." She looks around for approval and all heads nod in agreement.

"Well, I'm glad y'all like the place. As a member of the Mint Springs Historical Society, I'm happy my family's been able to help us out." Cade's in business meeting mode and I can't say I mind it. There's a confidence there that's usually not so fully on display. With the strong personalities his brothers are carrying around all day, there isn't always room for Cade to stand out. Here in this room he most certainly does.

"I think we had a list of questions for you—electrical, measurements, time constraints—things like that. Should we start with those now?" Molly's no slouch either when it comes to taking charge. I think she's normally a committee member and not so much of a leader, but given the opportunity she shines.

"Why don't we all go ahead and take a walk over to the big barn? That way y'all can see it in person. That'll be easier than listening to me drone on about the specifics." Several faces don't seem to mind listening to Cade talk and I get a little twinge of annoyance. Five minutes into things and I'm already getting territorial.

"That's a great idea." Molly's already packing up.

"If you think this building's impressive wait until you see the events barn. I think you'll be more than pleased with how that turned out." Cade's standing already, moving toward the door. "While y'all get organized, Faith, can I talk to you for a second in my office?"

"Of course." I feel a little like I've been called into the principal's office.

Cade holds out his arm like I don't know which direction to go and the formality of it is almost funny. I know exactly which office is his, thank you very much, although I can't tell any of the new members of the Mint Springs Historical Society the reason why. Once we go the four steps down the hall and Cade shuts the door behind us, his mouth is on mine.

"Sorry. I haven't seen you since this morning and it feels like a million years." He nuzzles my neck, letting all that delicious stubble rub along my throat.

"You never need to apologize for that. Listening to you in that meeting was making me hope we might get a second alone." I slide my arms around him and snuggle against his chest.

"Oh? Should I bring my laptop over to your place tonight and show you some spreadsheets?" The waggle of Cade's eyebrows has me giggling a little. "That sounds even less sexy when I say it out loud."

"I don't know it actually sounds a little dirty. Spreadsheets is a surprisingly suggestive word." Then we're both laughing probably loud enough for the ladies of the Historical Society to hear.

"We should start this tour, but now that I think about it, why don't we talk more about these *spreadsheets*—" Cade makes the word sound exceptionally dirty. "—at my house tonight? Will that mess up your morning if we sleep at my place?"

I'm still wrapped tightly around him, so I can feel the way he stiffens a little as he waits for my response. We've always stayed at my place because we didn't want Charlie to catch us, didn't want anyone to know about our secret relationship. Now, Cade's willing to take more risks and this is a big one. For both of us.

"Are you sure?" I whisper it into the cotton of his shirt.

"If you are."

"I'll pack a toothbrush."

## 35

*Cade*

"Are you sure this is a good idea?"

"No, but it's too late now." Faith brushes an imaginary piece of lint from my collar.

"Seriously?" My palms are already damp with sweat, having Faith confirm all the things I'm nervous about isn't helping the situation.

"I'm only kidding. You're so stiff. Relax."

I narrow my eyes at her. "Telling me to relax isn't going to help, not after giving me a heart attack."

"I'm only trying to lighten the mood. You know them; it'll be fine." Faith's voice isn't as confident as her words claim to be.

"Sure, but I'm not coming over to see if you want to come out and play baseball, Faith." I'm standing on the Bakers' front porch because I'm trying to date their daughter. Or maybe not *date*. A conversation about specifics probably would have been a good idea. But it really is too late now, because Faith's mother is opening the front door and I'm about to have to be on my best behavior.

An invitation to Sunday lunch is a bit more formal than I would have liked for things to be at this stage—too official. But if Faith and I are going to start letting people in on the fact that we're more than friends, we have to start somewhere. I probably should have mentioned my lack of experience with meeting the parents before I ended up in the front hallway, but there's no turning back now. I can't exactly run back down the front steps.

"Cade, welcome! Please come in." Faith's mother looks like the stereotypical 1950s housewife, straight out of *Southern Living*. She's wearing her pearls and a floral dress with a flowing skirt that swishes as she walks. It's been a while since I've been in the Baker house but I can see how Faith ended up so tidy. Her parents' house is spotless and I imagine that isn't just because they've been expecting company.

"These are for you." I hand Mrs. Baker the flowers I've been mangling. You'd think I was picking Faith up to take her to the prom the way my stomach's dancing around right now.

"Oh, these are lovely." She ignores the way I've rumpled the cellophane they're wrapped in. "How thoughtful. I'll run and put them in some water. Faith, why don't you bring Cade into the dining room?" I don't miss the look she gives Faith. She's impressed, or at least not horrified. Maybe the flowers have won me a few points.

The dining room is perhaps a more hostile audience. Faith's sisters are milling around, one of them straightening the silverware while the other two pretend they weren't even aware we've arrived.

"Oh, look who's here!" I've had a recent refresher course on Faith's sisters so I know that one's Hope. They've all kind of run together for me in the past. That won't do for trying to make a decent impression, so I'm armed today with enough facts about each of them to hopefully make conversation. This might not be an international summit, but I've prepared for it like it is.

"Yep. Here we are." Now it's Faith who seems nervous. I slide my arm around her waist in solidarity.

"We are all so glad you could make it for lunch today, Cade." This one's Charity, although the tone doesn't match her name. "It should liven things up *considerably*."

"Let's not get too lively." Faith's father's appearance has all the girls jumping. John Baker is a big man, the kind whose window you never wanted to launch a baseball through. He's also the kind whose daughter you don't defile and expect to live to tell the tale. I make sure to move my arm away from Faith's body in case that might put me on his bad side. "I need a few of you to go and help your mother."

Hope, Charity, and Constance all file out of the dining room but not before giving Faith few knowing glances. I imagine this is the time every teenaged boy who ever darkened the door of the Baker house dreaded. Even though I'm almost thirty years old I can feel a frisson of fear snake up my spine. John Baker could probably still take me in a fist fight. He's a farmer, for Pete's sake. He hasn't been sitting on his ass in an air-conditioned office all day; he's been out hauling fence posts and climbing on tractors. I make a mental note to never do anything that might convince him to test out his right hook.

"Cade, good to see you." He extends one weathered hand and I offer my own for a handshake. His grip further convinces me that doing right by Faith is absolutely necessary. Charlie might have thought he was putting the fear of God in Faith's potential suitors, but I'm convinced he had nothing to do with it. Two seconds with John Baker's hand wrapped around mine makes it all too easy to imagine that same hand around my neck. *Get it together, Cade. He's probably not going to kill you until after we eat.*

The return of the rest of Faith's family saves me from pissing my pants. It's much easier to make conversation as we all find our seats and start to negotiate the passing of platters and bowls. Faith's sisters are harmless for the most part, and the food is delicious. I'm not even exaggerating when I heap plenty of praise on the yeast rolls. No one cooks better than my aunts, but Faith's mother is giving them a run for their money. By the time dessert rolls around, I'm actually starting to enjoy myself.

"So, Cade, you've moved back here for good, is that right?" Faith's father's plate's been cleared and there's nothing to distract him.

"Yes, sir. We're all here permanently now."

"Permanently. Hmm. That's good." He seems to be looking at a spot above my right shoulder, thinking a little. "You looking to make some other permanent decisions?"

"Daddy, don't." Faith pats my leg under the table. "This is his first time over here. Don't turn it into the hot seat."

"I can't ask about Cade's plans?" He gives Faith an innocent look and I brace myself for the next question.

"Oh, Daddy's asking about plans?" Charity hustles back into the room carrying a chocolate cake on a glass stand. She puts it in the middle of the table and then shouts back toward the kitchen, "Hurry up. This is starting to get good."

I swallow. Faith and I haven't even had a discussion of plans and I don't relish the idea of doing it now in front of her family. "Well, the restaurant's open now and the next big piece of the business is the events space. We're planning on using that for the festival Faith and Molly are planning for the Historical Society." There. That's plans. That's the future.

Faith's returning sisters both look disappointed in my answer. We all know there was the implication of *personal* plans in the original question. I'm not here to ask for Faith's hand in marriage, though, I'm here because we're still feeling things out.

"But you do plan on settling down here, right?" Constance's question skirts around the subject.

"I am settled. I built a house. Mint Springs is home." Again, I deflect.

"And maybe you'd like to fill that house up with a bunch of kids? Eventually?" Hope gets closer to coming out and asking if I plan on marrying Faith and keeping her barefoot and pregnant.

"I haven't thought that far out." I can't look at Faith, can't risk seeing whatever emotion might be on her face. I'm lying and she'd be able to tell in a heartbeat, maybe she can already. I have thought about marriage and babies, and if I thought there was any way I could pull that off without things ending in disaster, Faith would be the person I'd probably like to try that with.

But I know how that would end, so I have no intention of even starting.

Luckily, my phone saves me from having to explain that answer. The 911 text from Cooper is enough of an excuse to let me kick that can down the road a little. I apologize for needing to eat and run and Faith's mother makes me promise I'll come again soon. But, if the look on Faith's face is any indication, I'm not so sure that's going to happen.

## 36

*Cade*

Cooper's 911 text turns out to be a non-issue. It saves my hide, most likely, but it's an easily fixable situation once I get myself back to our farm. The same can't be said for the way things unfold a few days later. I've been expecting Charlie to finally notice Faith's car parked in my driveway or to see us together now that we're not exactly sneaking around. Every time my brother enters a room, I get ready for a confrontation. It's bound to happen. Charlie's told me to leave Faith alone and I've done the opposite and then some. Eventually things will come to a head.

But Charlie never notices and the reason for that becomes painfully clear when he shows up drunk for family dinner a week or so later. While I've been waiting for the other shoe to drop, he's been destroying things with our executive chef. By the time the rest of us find out, it's too late. Jenna's on her way out of Georgia and our restaurant's in danger of failing. I'm furious with Charlie, and I'm not the only one. Even Sadie and Mae make sure he knows they think he's screwed up.

If there's anyone Charlie needs right now, it's Faith, but he's put a pretty good singe on that bridge, even if he didn't burn it down completely. And I have to admit, watching Faith try to help Charlie gets under my skin a little bit. Even after the way he's treated her, she's still willing to forgive him. That doesn't sit well with me, especially when his screw up means more time at work for me.

And less time with Faith.

"What time do you think you'll be home tonight?" She's pulling on her work clothes in the pink light of the sun starting to rise through my bedroom window.

"I have to take a turn in the restaurant." I prop myself up on my elbows so I can see her better. "It'll be late, unfortunately."

"Do you want me to stay over here? I can be here when you get home."

"No, don't do that. You'll be exhausted." Faith's early mornings do not mesh well with late nights running the front of the house at Sadie Mae's. Charlie has to be in the kitchen because there's no other choice, so Cooper, Chance, and I are now tasked with doing our best to pick up the slack. None of us is doing it well and we're all on edge.

"But if I sleep at my house, I won't get to see you for a few days. We're harvesting like crazy this week and I don't think I'll be able to get away." There's a frustration in Faith's voice that I easily recognize. I feel the same way.

"Then you'd better make this goodbye kiss count."

The string of curse words coming out of Cooper's mouth has me wishing I could turn right around and walk out of the restaurant.

"Sounds like you're having a great day."

Cooper curses again. "There is nothing in this place that's going right today."

"Then I can hardly wait to take over for you. Anything I should know about in advance or should I just wait until the problems are impossible to ignore?" I move behind the bar and let my oldest brother start his way toward the front door.

"There's a list back there somewhere. The big thing today is some kind of germ that's moving through the wait-staff. We'll be short again tonight. I've already had three of them call out sick. Keep calling Amanda. I can't get in touch with her and she's supposed to be on-call. If you can't find her, you'll end up waiting tables yourself." Cooper shakes his head. That wouldn't be the first time that's happened to one of us. "And see if you can take a look at next week's schedule, if you can. I didn't have a spare minute. Whose idea was it to open for lunch anyway? This is a nightmare."

"Go on home and let Hadley rub your feet," I tease.

"If anyone's getting a foot rub, it's the pregnant lady. But I've only got an hour before I have to be back over at Stolen Barn. The distillery isn't going to run itself while we're all trying to carry Charlie over here."

"How's he doing today?" I'm afraid to ask, but Charlie's mood can make or break a restaurant shift these days.

"He's miserable, of course. He misses Jenna and he's the only one to blame, really. At least he didn't break anything this afternoon. I hate to ever say this, but I'm hoping you have a slow night. Then he can leave early and Miguel can run the kitchen for a while. If we didn't have him, we'd really be in trouble." Cooper grimaces. "Now, if you'll excuse me, I'm going to go home and see if my wife even remembers me."

I wave him out the door. Around here if you don't leave when you have the opportunity, you can end up stuck here for the duration. I rifle around under the bar and find what passes for the staff schedule these days. Before Jenna left, Charlie was meticulous with the timing and organization of his staff, now I'm staring at a mangled sheet of notebook paper. At least Amanda's phone number is scribbled in the margins, otherwise I wouldn't know where to start looking for that. One thing's for sure: we can't keep limping along like this.

Normally, a crash from the kitchen and Charlie's unmistakable angry swearing would have had me running to see what was the matter. Today I barely even look up. If my brother needs a ride to the hospital, I trust he'll find a way to crawl out here. Eventually he comes out looking like he has all his fingers and toes. The bags under his eyes are as dark as I've ever seen them.

"Everything okay?" I already know the answer.

"It's fucking great, Cade. Couldn't be better." He grabs a glass from the drink station and fills it with water.

"She really got under your skin, huh?" I shouldn't poke the bear, but I can't resist.

Charlie glares at me, angrily raising the glass to his lips over and over again. "You think that's funny?"

"Of course not." None of this is funny, least of all the way our business is suffering.

"If you'd had what I had, you'd understand." Charlie puts the glass in the dish bin and gives me another glare. "But I guess here's another vote for your theory that everything ends. Maybe if I'd been more like you Jenna would still be here. I'd still be alone, though, because if I play it the way you prefer, she would only have been the chef here, right? No attachments."

I have to bite my tongue to keep from contradicting him. I understand what he thinks he had. I'm getting used to the way it feels to be able to roll over and watch Faith sleep, the way my entire inside lights up when she smiles at me. But he's right, that won't be around forever. It can't be and I'm not about to tell him about me and Faith right now. Not like this.

"If you want her back so badly, maybe you should do something about it." It's a dare I know he won't take me up on.

"Maybe I will."

## 37

*Faith*

I can't really blame Cade for being busy, but as the days apart turn into a week, I start to get cranky. I tell myself there's no reason to get all mopey about it and try to look on the bright side. At least Cade's pitching in when he's needed. At least he's dependable. Although sitting across from Molly at Ham & Eggs and having Cade be a no-show for our meeting of the Historical Society makes that one harder to believe.

"Do you think he's coming?" Molly looks at her watch. "Maybe we should go ahead and start without him. We've been waiting here for thirty minutes." She gives me a sad little frown. "Has he at least texted you?"

I look at my phone screen for the millionth time. "No. There's probably another emergency at the restaurant."

"We don't need him for this first part, anyway. And if we get something to eat that'll give him a few more minutes to get here." Molly's sunny disposition is getting on my nerves.

"Let's assume he isn't coming. We can go over the festival details without him. We need him for an update on the progress with the current owners of the mill, but maybe he can catch us up next time." Cade's part is still important and I have no idea how any of that is going. There's no mill to save if we haven't made progress on that front.

"That sounds good. Why don't we get you something to cheer you up a bit? How about an ice cream sundae? A milkshake? That's what I like when I'm having boy trouble." Molly scans the menu, looking only at the dessert section.

"I'm not having boy trouble."

"Or man trouble. Whatever you want to call it. When I have a lovers' quarrel with Brad, ice cream fixes me right up. Having him apologize is important too. An apology and ice cream. We can't get the apology right now, but the treat is easy enough." She looks across the diner for Debbie.

"Cade and I didn't have a fight." I cannot bring myself to say the words "lovers' quarrel."

"If you didn't before, I'm guessing you will tonight. You've got that angry little wrinkle you get when you're upset." She traces her finger in the space between her eyes and I scowl. "Yep, there it is again. When you see him tonight, he'll be in for it."

"I'm not going to see him tonight."

Molly's eyes widen. "Oh, it's like that is it? Then we'd better get the milkshake and the sundae. Possibly a piece of pie. Do you want peach or blueberry?" Her eyes turn back down toward the menu.

"No, there's nothing wrong." Not really. Not exactly. There's no way to explain this to Molly without looking like a love sick teenager. "Charlie messed things up with the chef and she left so now Cade's busy, that's all."

"I heard all about that. Who would have thought Charlie'd end up madly in love with that Jenna woman? Not me, I can tell you that. Is that what's got your panties in a wad,

Faith? I know you and Charlie have been friends for a while, but I thought you were stuck on Cade now." She leans over her glass of sweet tea and takes a long pull on her plastic straw while she waits for me to fill her in on all the details. Molly's worse than my sisters.

"I'm not stuck on him, whatever that means."

"You sure do seem like it. Everyone was talking about it after our last planning committee meeting. The way he looks at you—" Molly fans herself. "We all wondered if we should call the fire department."

"What? He does not. You did not." *Does he? Did they?* I thought we were still being a little discreet. I guess not.

"A five alarm fire, for sure, Faith. Don't pretend it isn't hot and heavy between the two of you. Sparks nearly fly off of you when you're together. And he's sweet. That's a great combination. Like me and Brad."

I don't recall ever thinking I had seen sparks flying when Molly and Brad were together, but I'm not exactly an expert about those kinds of things. One thing I'm starting to know for sure, though? "I don't think Cade's the kind to settle down."

"What? Why would you say that? That can't be right?"

"What can't be right?" Of course Debbie would choose this moment to appear at our table.

Molly doesn't even hesitate, she just starts filling Debbie in. "Faith thinks Cade's not the kind to settle down."

"Not the kind to settle down?" Debbie basically shouts it. "Why would you say that?" She leans on the edge of the table, and I know she's not going anywhere until I spill my guts.

"Things he's said." I don't need to go into detail.

"We need details," Molly says and Debbie agrees. "Specifics."

I sigh. I am terrible at girl talk, but I'm even worse at figuring out all this cryptic relationship talk. Maybe Molly and Debbie can help me decipher it. Maybe I've been reading Cade's reactions all wrong. "When anyone asks him about his plans, Cade only talks about the business."

Molly chews on her bottom lip a little. "Go on."

"And he seems very attentive when we're together, but he never mentions anything about the future." The easy smiles I hope to see at this confession aren't appearing. "At first I thought it was because we were trying to keep things a little secret—"

"You two did a terrible job of that, by the way," Debbie volunteers.

"But now I don't know what it is. He's busy is all, maybe." I wait for them to tell me not to worry, but instead Debbie slides into the booth next to Molly.

"What about when you—" Molly leans in and whispers. "—spend the night? Do you leave things at his house? Did you offer him a drawer at yours?"

"Am I supposed to do that?" This is news to me.

"It is a good test," Debbie agrees. "Has he left anything behind? A toothbrush? A T-shirt?"

I think back. "I don't think so." I'm getting the tiniest pit in the bottom of my stomach.

"Do you even really want it to get serious, though?" Molly asks. "Sometimes casual is fun." Her expression does not make it look like she really believes this.

"I would like to have kids some day, and it's not like we're babies." I might have been a little green when it comes to relationships and sex a few months ago, but that doesn't mean I don't want to keep things moving forward. Sleep-overs and stolen moments are great, but that's not all I want.

"Right." Molly folds her hands on the tabletop. "If you

think he's not going to be able to give you what you want, you can't wait around and hope to find out. You're going to have to come out and ask him."

Debbie nods. "You can try to beat around the bush, but you'll only waste time and you might end up with your heart broken."

I consider this. A broken heart doesn't seem like something I want, but I've been pining after Cade forever. Imagining him moving on without me, even if that doesn't mean he's marrying someone else, already hurts.

That must be written all over my face because Molly and Debbie go silent. When Debbie stands back up it's with a face too solemn to be thinking I've got a great chance at getting out of this unscathed.

"I think we're going to need an ice cream sundae, a chocolate milkshake, and a slice of blueberry pie." Molly recites our order like she's reading the eulogy at a funeral.

"A la mode?" Debbie doesn't seem the least bit surprised.

"I think we're going to need it."

## 38

*Cade*

Finally we're all in the mood to celebrate.

After working ourselves nearly to death, things look to be getting back to normal. Well, as normal as we can probably get with all these balls in the air. Charlie's patched things up with Jenna and, hopefully, all our lives are about to get a little less interesting. Predictable sounds pretty damn good to me right about now.

Something else that sounds good? Uninterrupted time with my best girl. I can't get that this second, unfortunately, but I fully intend to take Faith to bed and keep her there as long as her farming schedule will allow as soon as I get the opportunity. And I think that might be able to happen tonight, right after we let my Aunt Mae blow out the candles on her birthday cake.

We're setting up for the party at Sadie Mae's, another responsibility that's been driving me crazy for the past two weeks. Mae had wanted a raucous party and we've got the perfect place to throw one, but that all takes planning and organizing and Charlie's been in no condition to take point on that. Or on anything for that matter. After yesterday though, I'm feeling confident he'll be able to start pulling his weight again and I can get back to crunching the numbers. I've got mill business to get back to, too. But before I worry about any of that, I intend to enjoy myself tonight.

The giant ice sculpture we ordered from Atlanta is being wheeled in when I see Faith coming through the front door. She's carrying a crate of vegetables for tonight's dinner and I rush to take it from her.

"Hey." I lean forward and kiss her but she pulls away before I can really give her more than a peck.

"That's only part of the order. I'll run out and get the rest." She's turning her back on me before I have a chance to say anything.

"I'll get it. How many more boxes are there? We can walk and talk." I have to almost run to catch up with her.

"I don't have much time to waste."

*Since when has spending time together been a waste?* "Okay." I help her haul the rest of the produce in. "These look great. You're growing patty pan squash now?"

"We've been growing them." Faith's answers are curter than I'm used to, but she's been as busy as I have—maybe more. I can't expect her to fawn all over me when she's working. A little interest would be nice, though.

I get a warning bell in the back of my mind. Just a tiny tinkling, but enough to have me off-center. I ignore it and try again to get my hands on Faith. I'm nearly free from the purgatory that has been Sadie Mae's for the last few weeks and I can't keep all that exuberance to myself.

She isn't taking the bait, though. Faith keeps right on moving, handing me the invoice and dusting her hands off on the front of her overalls. "I need to take a look at those beds out back before I go. I'll see you tonight." It's a dismissal. I could offer to come with her out back door, try to sneak in some smooching against the wall the way we used to, but she doesn't seem interested.

Things seem off, but how could they not be? Faith and I haven't been able to connect in weeks. Tonight, all that tension will be gone. Tonight, I'm making up for lost time.

I wait and wait for Faith to arrive. The party's been in full swing for hours and the rest of my family is hooting and hollering. We've got a live band and plenty of people are taking advantage of the chance to dance. Even though Hadley's been complaining about her swollen ankles, she's begging Cooper to swing her around the dance floor. Chance and Lily are shaking their asses out there too, and I wish I could join them. But I want to do it with Faith, not alone. Not being the third wheel.

"She still isn't here?" Mae comes up beside me as I continue to watch the door and nurse my drink.

"Who?"

She rolls her eyes. "I may be old, but I'm not blind, Cade."

"I thought you were turning twenty-one today?" It's what we've been saying about Sadie and Mae's birthdays for years now, but it seems less funny to her tonight.

"Did you tell her how much you were looking forward to seeing her tonight? Faith might need a little encouragement."

"How did you know?" I probably shouldn't even bother to ask. If she knew when I hid that pack of cigarettes in the barn when I was thirteen, she knows about everything. Those cigarettes made me sick anyway. I'd hacked and coughed trying to learn how to smoke them, but Mae hadn't given me a lecture. She'd let me figure out all on my own that smoking wasn't for me. And they'd been menthol. Barf.

"You don't hide it as well as you think. And I don't think you should be hiding it. Charlie'll get his nose bent out of shape, but he'll get over it. A girl like Faith is worth that."

"She's worth it, all right." I look toward the front door again.

"Why in the world do you sound so sad about it?" Mae's eyes are full of concern.

"Because I know how it'll end up. No one stays happy for long." Mae will understand this. She never ended up with the love of her life. She stayed here in Mint Springs, living with her sister. My grandmother died and left my grandfather alone. My parents divorced and now they hate each other. There are countless other stories like this; I've got data to back up the way I feel.

"You can't think that." She's genuinely surprised. "Look at your brothers. They're happy."

"For now." I know this isn't a short-term experiment. In a few years Cooper, Chance, and Charlie might not be smiling the way they are now.

"You be careful, Cade. Those kinds of thoughts become reality. When Faith finally walks through that door, if you're doom and gloom, that's what you're going to get." I half expect Mae to wag a stern finger at me, but she's probably saving that for later. "Now if you'll excuse me, rumor has it that ice sculpture can double as a luge for vodka shots."

That at least gets me to smile. I should have known Mae wasn't asking for that giant hunk of frozen water just for aesthetics. I'm still shaking my head as she walks away, laughing a little to myself. But I straighten up real quick when Faith materializes in my line of sight. Hells bells, she looks good. There's no one who can compare to Faith as far as I'm concerned, and there probably never will be.

As she walks toward me, my smile only widens, and as I wrap my arms around her, I can feel the tension of the last few weeks leave my body. It surprises me enough to pull back a little. I've been needing a good dose of Faith and all that sunshine. I'm so tempted to kiss her, onlookers be damned. Just pull her in close and claim her mouth for everyone to see. *That's why these feelings are dangerous. They trick you into doing things that you might regret later. They make you forget the consequences.*

Faith is the one to put a little space between us, and I'm grateful she's got a clear head. She's saving me from myself right now. Maybe saving herself too.

"Can we talk for a minute?" Her face is serious.

"Of course."

"Somewhere more private?" It doesn't sound like an invitation to sneak off to my office and get naked.

"Sure." She lets me take her hand, but something's off.

I have a feeling I'm not going to like whatever Faith's about to tell me.

## 39

*Faith*

*I have to do it before I lose my nerve.*

I've said it to myself a million times already tonight. It didn't help me get out of my house any faster, though. Instead, it made me spend an extra hour making sure I got my hair just right. It didn't light a fire under my butt once I got in the car, either. I drove around town, taking the long way here, telling myself I didn't want to be one of the first guests to arrive at Mae's big party. And it didn't exactly make me rush from the parking lot, even if I knew Cade was waiting for me a few feet away. I sat there, watching everyone else go in, my hands shaking so badly I had to keep them clenched around the steering wheel.

I don't know why I'm so nervous. Molly's assured me things are going to go my way. She's coached me on what—and what not—to say. I'll ask Cade about the future, and he'll say what I want to hear. His hesitation has only been about our situation. He's not avoiding it at all. He's been focused on the present, because we were trying to stay under the radar. Maybe he'll even laugh about me ever worrying about it. He doesn't need to say he wants to be with me forever. He only needs to say forever's in his vocabulary. That it might be a possibility. Then this knot that's been twisting and tightening in my stomach will finally go away.

He looks happy to see me, at least. When I come into Sadie Mae's, the party's already in full swing. There's a band playing—saxophone, trumpet, the whole deal—so the noise level isn't great for a serious conversation. Everyone else is dancing. I must have already missed the food. Cade isn't shy about hugging me, which I take as another positive sign. He holds me longer than necessary to be friendly, and he doesn't seem to mind who notices.

"Can we talk for a minute?" Why do I think I might cry? I'm not one to start the waterworks for no reason. A hammer to the thumb? Maybe. A misplaced fish hook? Sure. But a boy? Never.

"Of course." And then Cade stands there, apparently thinking we can go ahead and get this conversation started right here.

"Somewhere more private?"

There's a hint of a smile again, but then Cade's forehead wrinkles. He's starting to realize I'm not talking about the kind of privacy he likes. "Sure."

He reaches for my hand—I put that in the positive column. Maybe if I had more experience with this I'd know how to read him better. I know *him*, or at least I thought I did. But I've never had to have a talk like this. Usually my relationships—the few of them I've had—tend to fizzle out. I haven't wanted more from any of them, and they haven't bothered to find out why. I've always assumed that feeling must have been mutual. That's never made me think my heart might come out of my chest, never made me wish I could have a shot of something for a little liquid courage, never made me consider if throwing up on someone's shoes might be a real possibility. But all those things are happening now.

Because after I say what I've come to say, it could go either way. It will be up to Cade, and there's not much I can do to change that.

We end up out back by the herb garden, and the smell of basil and thyme soothes me a little. Nothing bad can happen in a garden, can it? It's almost like a talisman. He won't reject me out here with all these plants looking on.

"What's up?" Cade keeps holding my hand, and I don't dare let him go.

"I need to ask you something." My voice shakes.

"That doesn't sound good." Cade frowns. "What's wrong?"

"Why don't we ever... Why don't *you* ever..." I'm having trouble even getting any of it out. "What are we doing, Cade?"

"We're standing out here in the dark wasting time we could be spending dancing at my great-aunt's birthday party." He means it as a joke, but I can't even pretend to crack a smile.

"Are we just wasting all our time, though? Do you see a future in this?" *Breathe, Faith.*

"Are you talking about this?" Cade gestures with his free hand into the space between us.

I can only nod.

"That's a big question, considering we've barely even gone public. Charlie still doesn't know and... I think that might be jumping the gun a little bit, don't you think? We've got plenty of time before that conversation." The words sound almost right, but his posture's all wrong, and Cade's grip on my hand has tightened enough to have my fingers tingling.

"Do we, though? Because whenever you talk about the future, you only talk about work. You never mention anything personal. To anyone, Cade. Not just to me." I can feel myself standing on the edge of a cliff, recklessly flinging myself over to the rocks down below. Maybe Molly was wrong, and I should have left things alone for a bit longer. I like what I have with Cade.

I just want more.

He releases my hand and it drops to my side, my fingers cold even though the night's still warm. "If you're asking me to tell you I'm planning our wedding, I can't do that, Faith." Cade's eyes meet mine and then pan to the ground. "I'm not sure I'll ever be planning a wedding and a family. With anyone."

The shock of his words knocks me back a step. "What does that even mean?"

"It means I don't think that's the life I'm going to have. It doesn't make any sense to lie." He takes a deep breath. "If I was going to give that a try... I can't promise you something I know I can't deliver."

"Why would you ever start anything with me, then?" There's anger creeping into my voice.

"I was weak, I guess. I've always wanted you, Faith, even if I know I shouldn't. Hell, I promised Charlie I'd leave you alone years ago and not even that stopped me." He reaches for my hand, but I pull it away.

"He made you promise that?"

"Of course, you're the little sister he never had." Cade acts like that's the most reasonable thing in the world.

"But that doesn't mean he gets to decide my life. He went behind my back and orchestrated things. And you...you think that's fine?" I'm yelling now, attracting attention from the parking lot as some of the guests get in their cars to leave.

"He thought he was protecting you," Cade argues. "I might have done the same thing."

"He was protecting me from *you*, Cade. *From you*." I want to scream up at the sky, want to punch Cade right in that perfect chin of his.

"Maybe he was right to."

"Maybe he was!" I scream it at him right before I turn on my heel and walk away. There's a little crowd now on the edge of the parked cars. Charlie's walking up right as my feet hit the gravel.

"What's going on out here?" The question's directed at me, but I don't slow down. I'm not about to explain anything to him.

"Kiss my ass, Charlie." There are several gasps behind me, but I ignore them all. Right now, *everyone* can kiss my ass, even if means I'm going to hell for thinking so.

## 40

*Cade*

Charlie's blocking my way into Sadie and Mae's house when I show up the next night for dinner. I glare up at him standing on the top stair, keeping me from getting inside.

"You're not coming in here until you clear a few things up for me first."

"Then I guess I'm not going in." I turn around and start to march back to the gravel road. I walked here, so I'll just walk my ass back home. I'm not about to let Charlie put me through an interrogation.

His footsteps crunch behind me, jogging to catch up. "I'm serious, Cade. We need to talk."

"So talk." I keep walking.

"What was going on last night with you and Faith?"

I increase my pace, and do my best not to look at him. "Did you ask her?"

"I tried. She told me to kiss her ass, and now I can't get in touch with her."

I can't hold in my startled laugh. *Faith said that?* She's angrier than I thought. *That's my girl.* I let the thought sit there for a bit before I remind myself Faith isn't my girl. Not at all. Not anymore.

"I'm glad you think it's so funny. Maybe you can tell me why the two of you were screaming at each other behind Sadie Mae's? I'd like a straight answer." Charlie grabs my upper arm and forces me to a stop. "Tell me right now before I lose my temper."

"We weren't screaming, and it's none of your business." I turn around and head back to Mae and Sadie's. "You know what? I'm not skipping dinner just to keep the peace."

Charlie follows me, his boots kicking rocks along as he tries to keep up. I bound up the front stairs and through the front door before he can say another word. Using the rest of my family as human shields may be cowardly, but I'm doing it anyway.

"Well, there they are." Sadie's putting pork chops on the table. "We thought we were going to have to eat without you."

"When you've made pork chops? I wouldn't miss that for anything." Not even of it means staring at Charlie's stupid face all night. I give Sadie a kiss on the cheek. "Have you recovered from last night?" If I pretend everything's fine, maybe it will be.

"That was one heck of a party. I'm feeling fine today, but Mae was dragging this morning. I had to feed the chickens on my own. She got too familiar with that ice sculpture, if you ask me." Sadie winks.

"That thing was dangerous," Chance concedes. He's coming to the table carrying a bowl of butter beans. "Where'd you take off to last night? We could have used your help pushing that thing outside. It was a mess."

"I got partied out. Left a little early."

Charlie shoots me a look from across the room.

"We handled it fine," Cooper reassures me, bringing in a plate of biscuits. Hadley's tagging along behind him.

"I left a little early too. I cannot party the way I used to." She pats her belly. "This little guy got tired of the dancing."

"But we tore it up for a bit there, baby." Cooper leans over to give Hadley a kiss, and my gut twists. It's a mixture of emotions: sadness, jealousy, and regret.

"We all did." Lily's smiling up at Chance, and that's like a knife in my heart. "We missed you on the dance floor, Cade. It was one big, embarrassing Allen family conga line at one point."

"He was too busy yelling at Faith to make time for dancing." Charlie's at the table now, and back to pushing his luck.

"You and Faith have a fight? I thought that was going well." Lily gives the side of Chance's arm a smack to shut him up, but it's too late.

"*What* was going well?" Charlie's question goes unanswered in an uneasy silence.

"Why don't we all sit down before the food gets cold." This time it's Mae to the rescue, coming into the dining room wearing her tiara from last night.

Chairs scrape as we negotiate fitting around the table. Dishes get passed, and my fight with Faith gets forgotten.

"Did Jenna already leave for Boston?" Cooper asks around a mouthful of beans.

"This morning," Charlie answers. "But she'll be back as soon as she can get things organized." He's got happiness spilling out of him right now, basically bouncing in his seat thinking about having Jenna back here. I don't blame him; that's been a hard thing to make happen and, despite how I feel about him in this moment, I hope it lasts for a while.

"So I guess you've got a little time on your hands." I

mean to just think it, but it comes out of my mouth before I can slide a bite of pork chop in.

Charlie looks at me quizzically. "Still pretty busy."

"I was thinking that might mean you finally had some time for Faith. Makes sense why you're suddenly giving a shit." I take a bite of my biscuit as the entire table falls silent. Not only have I brought up the subject everyone was gracious enough to help me avoid, I've cussed. At the dinner table.

"What is that supposed to mean?" Charlie's stare is steely, much more menacing than before.

"When Jenna's in the mix, you don't have time for her, but now you'll jump back into her life for a bit. While you're bored. Then you can jet on out again. Model friendship." I cannot seem to shut my mouth, and my stare is as serious as Charlie's.

Not a soul is eating as Charlie and I keep our eyes locked across the table.

"I'd advise you to keep your nose out of places it doesn't belong, Cade." Charlie's nostrils flare. He and I both know starting a fist fight at Sadie and Mae's dinner table would mean a hell of a lot more than just no dessert for a while, but he looks like he still might come over the table top.

"You think that's not my business?" I challenge, rising up taller in my chair and leaning forward. "You think you get to do whatever you want and still have her just hanging around, begging for your scraps of attention?"

"Are you talking about me or are you talking about yourself, Cade? From where I'm sitting, it sure does look like Faith's fine with me, but you're the one she's got a problem with."

Charlie's right, of course, and this makes my blood boil. I imagine myself flipping the table over like in one of those action movies. With all the anger running through me right now, it'd probably be easy. I won't do that, though; I would never do that. Instead I blink a few times, letting the reality of the situation sink in. Faith is mad at Charlie, but she'll most likely get over it. He'll be back in her good graces, and I'll still be standing on the outside. And, yes, somewhere in the back of my mind I know I chose that, but right now I still want it to be Charlie's fault.

"You want to step outside?"

Charlie laughs. "What's your plan, Cade? You're going all Wild West? We're going to fight for her?" The laugh is more surprised than dismissive, and Charlie doesn't look particularly interested in leaving the table.

The sound of my chair scraping against the floor has all my brothers standing. Cooper and Chance both look at me like I've lost my mind.

"Boys," Sadie warns. "Don't you dare."

"Thanks for dinner." It's all the manners I've got left in me. "I'm leaving."

Once I'm out the door the cool night air helps calm me down a little bit. Charlie had been sarcastic about fighting over Faith, but I would have gone outside in a heartbeat. I'd be willing to scrap with my own brother over her, but what's that worth? I haven't been willing to fight for her in the way that counts.

And maybe I never will.

## 41

*Faith*

Now that I don't have to fit Cade into my schedule, I've got more hours in the day than I realized. Instead of rushing back from his place or wishing he could stay longer at mine, I'm bounding out of bed and ploughing through my day. I've got my bed all to myself and only me to answer to.

Only I'm not sleeping. I'm up all night, missing the sound of Cade's heart beating steadily in his chest. I used to fit perfectly there, with his arm wrapped around me, and now I can't fall asleep without that stupid thumping. The ticking of the clock on my bedside table is no substitute, even though I hear the passing of every second. If this is what a broken heart feels like, then I've been smarter than I thought making sure I never came close to love all these years. How do people survive this?

I give the Sadie Mae's delivery to the new driver—there's no way I'm going to risk seeing Cade, especially if I can't control the situation. Having him pop up as I'm dragging a case of cabbages through the front door would possibly have me bursting into tears. My father had given me a look when I'd told him I'd be letting Andy take care of things, but he hadn't asked any questions.

The Historical Society is harder to manage. Molly has the next planning meeting at her house, and I debate pretending to be sick. A convincing cough should be easy to pull off, although I hate leaving Molly with no help in that room full of piranhas. In the end, Cade makes it easy for me, pulling out an excuse of his own and skipping the sweet tea and conversation at Molly's.

I get a few pitying looks as I walk through Molly's front door. I guess everyone has heard about our not-so-private discussion outside Mae's birthday party. Walking right back out the front door seems like the best idea I've had all day, but Molly intercepts me before I can turn around.

"Nope, nope, nope. The only way around town gossip is through it, Faith," she whispers to me, putting my upper arm in a vise grip and pulling me inside. "You have to hold your head up high and keep a smile on your face." She shows me a surprisingly frightening grimace. I'm pretty sure making a face like that won't help.

"It doesn't bother me," I lie, even though I'm gritting my teeth.

"Oh, please. Getting dumped by Cade Allen would have leveled any of these bitches, pardon my French. I'm sure you're a little banged up. It'll pass. In the meantime, we have a party to plan."

"It's a *festival*, Molly." I manage a tiny smile. "And he didn't dump me."

"Well, then get in there and act like it."

After a few probing questions about Cade's empty chair, Molly and I get the meeting underway. The committees are making progress, and the festival is really coming together. It does feel good to be out doing something other than work or moping, even if it does require me to plaster on a smile. I'm not used to having to fake it, and an hour later I'm exhausted.

"There, you did it. We should finish these cookies to celebrate." Molly comes back from escorting the last of our committee members out the door and shoves a plate of snickerdoodles at me.

"No, thanks. I'm going to need to get going." After all, I've got an empty house to get back to.

"Oh, come on, have one." Molly aims the plate at me again. "I need to pretend we're still working so Brad will keep entertaining the kids for a bit longer." She flops down in one of her fancy dining room chairs and takes a bite of the cookie in her hand. "Don't make me eat alone."

"Fine, but only one." I take one of the sugary discs from the plate and sink my teeth into it. "These are pretty good."

"Martha Stewart's recipe." Molly lets her arms dangle over the armrests, sprawled out like a starfish. "Sometimes you just need a little sugar."

The cookie *is* making me feel better. I take another bite and chew. "Cade is missing out."

"He sure is. But if he can't see what a catch you are, then you're better off without him." Molly raises a fist in the air.

"I was talking about the cookie, but that, too. Thanks for being so nice about it, Molly. About everything." I mean it. Molly's had every opportunity to put me in my place. I wasn't the most gracious partner when we started this project, and she's never thrown that in my face.

"I was a little worried you'd be mad."

"Mad? At you? About what?" I reach for a second cookie.

"About the advice I gave you. If I hadn't told you to talk to Cade, you might still be together." Molly's mouth turns down. "I felt like I pushed you a little."

"I probably needed a little push. And you were right—if Cade wasn't on the same page as me, it was better to find out now." I've never had a friend to talk to about things like this. Molly and I might be opposites in many ways, but she's turning out to be a good listener.

"He'll come around." Molly nods her head like it's a done deal.

"I don't know about that. He seemed pretty sure of his decision." I shrug. "Nothing I can do about us having different ideas about the future."

"Still, he's crazy about you, Faith. Maybe he hasn't said it in so many words, but he's got some strong feelings. It's hard to think those would disappear." She gives me the same look my mother gives me when she's sure she's right.

"Then I guess we'll see, but I'm not holding out too much hope. I think Cade and I are over."

"It still hurts, though, doesn't it?"

"It does." I close my eyes. I'm not sure when this ache is going to go away.

"You've got strong feelings too." Molly's mouth turns down again. "Oh, Faith."

I frown too, because it's hard to think those feelings are going to just disappear.

## 42

*Cade*

There's not much I can do to ease the ache in my chest, but keeping moving helps a little. I get back into my routine: running around the farm in the morning and burying myself in work for the rest of the day. I try to avoid Charlie, which is hard since we eat dinner together almost every night and a good deal of my work issues have to do with Sadie Mae's. I use Cooper and Chance to run interference, pretending I've got to be somewhere—anywhere else—to avoid seeing Charlie in person.

And I avoid Faith at all costs. I can't risk running into her at the restaurant, so it makes sense to keep my distance. I set up an imaginary line in my head and do my best not to cross it. That means no Historical Society, of course, but I can't exactly just forget about the promises I've made there. I made those to Molly, too. I might not be able to give Faith the life she wants, but I can give her the mill. I can try to live up to my word, even if I haven't been doing that lately.

"This all looks good, Cade, but I'm not sure we're going to go in this direction."

"What?" I sit up a little straighter in the uncomfortable fake leather chair in Samuel Cutter III's real estate office. He's been handling the sale of the mill for his family and, up until now, I thought we were full steam ahead. "What does that mean?"

"It means that developer came through with his offer, and it makes the idea of settling for what you're offering seem like a dumb move." He shrugs his shoulders and slides the papers I've given him back across the desk. "I'm not sure I can make this idea of yours work."

"But we've been hammering this out for weeks now. You're telling me a higher offer is all it takes for you to back out of this?" I stare at Sammy in disbelief. "I thought your family was interested in saving the mill—in having it become a landmark."

"Some of them are, sure, but the rest of us know you can't pay the bills on goodwill, Cade."

"We're giving you a fair price."

"But are you giving me *this* price?" Sammy slides another piece of paper toward me with a number so high written on it I have to look twice.

"We can't possibly give you that much. That's what they're offering you?" I blink down at the paper. There's no way we could raise that kind of money, not with all the harvest festivals in the world. "What are they going to build that they think they can make a profit after spending that kind of money?"

"It's going to be a subdivision, I think. And property values around here are going up. I have you and your brothers to thank for that, actually. You're making it look like this area's up and coming, I guess. They're figuring if you can get people to pay for dinner at a fancy restaurant, then you can convince them to buy bigger houses."

Sammy smiles at me. "That part's not my problem, luckily."

"But they'll have to tear it all down to be able to fit enough houses on the land. You get that, don't you?" I'm flabbergasted. This is the exact opposite of the things we've been talking about. Up until now it seemed the Cutters wanted to pass the mill on but couldn't figure out a way to do it. Selling the land this way makes it all but assured the buildings get leveled and the history gets lost.

"Again, that might be the price of progress. You understand that. Y'all tore down that old barn to build your distillery. That was history, wasn't it?" He leans back in his chair like he's just made the winning move in a chess game.

"We didn't tear it down. The existing structure couldn't be used. We actually repurposed it. All of the original barn wood is still there, but it's part of the new building. Believe me, if we could have used the original building, we would have." It had been hard to watch the old barn be dismantled. That was wood milled from our land—at Cutter's mill, no less—and put together by my grandfather with his own hands. But that's family history, and although as Allens we've done our best to save the things that matter to us as a family, the mill is *community* history. Mint Springs doesn't need another subdivision, not at this expense.

"I could maybe talk to them about using the old stuff that's there, but I can't make them do any of that. They'll want to get started ASAP and getting into a back and forth with them about how to run their business won't be good business for me." Sammy shrugs again like it's out of his hands. "Sorry, Cade. I think we're going to pass.

"Pass?" I can feel the panic rising in me. "After a two-minute discussion?"

"No use in dragging it out. I can give you a few days to

come up with a better offer, but that's the best I can do." Sammy stands, dismissing me. "I look forward to seeing what you come up with." He extends his hand, and I think about refusing to shake it.

"A few more days? Our fundraiser isn't for two weeks. How are we supposed to come up with our counteroffer in a few days?" I try to appeal to his sense of pride. "This isn't about money, Sam. It's about cementing your family's legacy in Mint Springs."

"Everything's about money, Cade. And I'd rather cement my legacy with a little more green." He extends his hand farther. "I'll give y'all a few more days."

I shake his hand with a little more force than necessary. He's backed me into a corner, and he knows it. What he doesn't know, however, is that the desperation I'm feeling isn't about some pissing contest. He thinks we're sparring over business, trying to get the best deal. But I couldn't give a rat's ass about any of that. I'm fighting for the chance to show Faith I'm still worth something, that I'm not all talk. Sammy's making that impossible, and I'm going to have to stand in front of her and let her down. Again.

## 43

*Faith*

"What do you mean 'Sam rejected our offer?'" Molly's voice is loud enough for all of Ham & Eggs to hear.

"They've got some big developer offering to buy it for significantly more money." Cade doesn't try to soften the blow, and I'm sure my shock shows.

"I don't understand. I thought the Cutters wanted to preserve the mill, too." I make the mistake of looking at his face and have to turn my head. It's the first time we've seen each other in person since our fight, and I'm having trouble looking him in the eye. It makes it too hard not to beg him to forget everything I said and go back to the way things were before.

Cade clears his throat. "I thought they did, too, but Sammy seems to think they're better off going with the highest bidder."

"The highest bidder?" Molly's screech has people turning to look at our booth.

"We won't be able to compete with the highest bidder." I

let out a frustrated sigh. "And even if we raise a ton of money at the festival, it won't be nearly enough."

"We don't know that just yet, Faith," he cautions. "But Sammy's only giving us a few days to make a counteroffer."

"The festival isn't for two more weeks. How will we even know how much we have to offer?" I look at Cade like he might have the answer, but he can't predict the future any more than I can.

"I don't know."

"Then there's no reason to have the festival at all," Molly laments. "We should just cancel it before we get any further along."

"It's already too late to cancel it." I shake my head. We've booked performers and opened it up for vendors. Canceling it now will only hurt them. "Even if we can't save the mill, we can use that money for other projects. We have to go ahead with the festival, even if we have to tell people the reason for fundraising has changed."

"People won't like that." Molly might be right, but people won't like us canceling at the last minute either.

"We don't have much choice." I take a sip of my coffee and appreciate the bitterness in my mouth. Just like everything else, this is turning to crap right before my eyes.

"I'm still trying to come up with a way to make this work, Faith." Cade doesn't sound hopeful.

"Maybe this wasn't meant to be." I'm talking about more than the mill, and he knows it. His face falls, and I have to focus on the wall again.

～

"You look like someone just ran over your dog." My father means it as a joke, but I can't even fake a smile.

"We don't have a dog." I begged and begged for one when I was younger, but Charity's allergic, so there was never a puppy at the Baker house.

"Things can't be that bad. Come and take a look at these seedlings. Remember how we thought those seeds from last year were bunk? They've sprouted." He gestures to the black plastic tray in front of him. "Just needed a little patience."

I walk across the greenhouse floor and come up beside him. Sure enough, there are a few tiny green specks poking out from the seed-starting mix in the container. "That's great, Daddy."

"I was expecting more enthusiasm than that." He raises an eyebrow at me. "You really are having a bad day."

Bad day, bad week, bad month... I could keep going. "I've had better. Our deal to buy the mill looks to be falling apart."

"I'm sorry to hear that. Anything I can do?" Of course my father wants to try to help.

"No." I make myself busy with the seedling trays in front of me. Between the plants we intended to sell at the festival, and the ones we'd already promised for the local nursery, my father and I have been spending more time in the greenhouse than usual. More fall crops need to be started, or we won't be able to fill our vegetable orders.

"That sounds pretty definitive." He's teasing me a little, trying to cheer me up, but it seems for once not even my Daddy can make things right.

"It is. Sometimes there's just nothing you can do to fix things." I give a sigh of resignation that has my father laughing.

"That's the kind of drama I might expect from one of your sisters, but not from you, Faith. From you, I'd expect sleeves being rolled up. You've never backed down from a challenge."

"Maybe I've learned that not every obstacle is something to spend my energy on." Sounds more jaded than I intended, but that might be the new me. The older and wiser Faith Baker, resigned to her fate as a spinster farmer out here in the middle of nowhere Georgia.

"I can agree with you on that in principle, but life isn't all about theory." He puts his trowel down on the makeshift table in front of him. We've got plywood on sawhorses now that we've run out of room on the real counters. "But I think we're talking about more than the mill right now, aren't we?"

I keep my eyes on my work, spreading the potting mix so evenly you'd think there was an award for it. "No."

"This wouldn't be about a certain Allen boy? One who came to Sunday lunch but now has disappeared off the face of the earth and taken your smile with him?"

"He hasn't disappeared." It would have been easier if he had. Then I wouldn't have to try and avoid his stupid face all day long. "We just aren't spending as much time together."

"Hmmm. That have anything to do with a little argument y'all had at Miss Mae's birthday party?"

I startle. "Who told you we had an argument?"

"Your sisters have been talking about it nonstop, among other people. News travels fast around here. Heard you used some colorful language." He's smiling a little, oblivious to the fact that finding myself the subject of local gossip is making me dizzy.

"I only said ass, and I had a good reason."

"A good enough reason to stop seeing Cade?"

"That wasn't my decision to make."

"So that's that? You seemed to really like him. Have for a while, I reckon." My father's stare is serious now, his hands braced on the plywood tabletop. "I would think that wouldn't be over after one disagreement."

"It was more than a disagreement; it was a fundamental difference of opinion. He and I want different things, and in this instance it's not something we can compromise on." I lift my chin. I know enough to know I'm right. Cade wants casual and I want more, and we can't move beyond that.

"A fundamental difference of opinion?" My father scratches the scruff on his chin. "That does sound serious."

"It was. It is."

"I've had those before. Sometimes it turned out what I thought was an insurmountable problem was only a little bump in the road." He tilts his head, looks at me like he's solved everything.

"This isn't some trivial thing, Daddy. I want to eventually settle down, make a life with someone. Cade doesn't want that and he claims he never will. That's more than a bump." I try to keep my voice from wavering.

"Y'all been discussing that kind of thing?" He's less surprised than I would have expected.

"Not exactly. The first time I asked about it was at Mae's party."

"Ah." My father nods his blond head. "And that was the disagreement. Makes sense."

"I got tired of not knowing. So I asked." I'm less sure about my tactics now, but at the time it made sense.

"Backed him into a corner a little bit, though. Seeing as how he thought he was coming to his aunt's party and got blindsided by a relationship conversation. And a serious one at that. Probably didn't have much time to think."

"But he shouldn't need time to think. He should *know*, Daddy. If he doesn't know, then I don't need to waste any more time." I grit my teeth in frustration.

"Sometimes you have to give people a little time to adjust their thinking."

"What is there for Cade to adjust? He thinks he'll *never* want to have the kind of life I want. He isn't going to make a one-eighty." I fist my hands in exasperation. "You don't understand."

"I understand better than you know. Imagine this: a grubby farmer falls in love with the local beauty queen." My father looks at me and raises his eyebrows, moves his hand through the air like he's getting ready to do a dramatic reading. "Everybody knew that was never going to work. Heck, *I* knew that wasn't going to work. I couldn't imagine your mother, with her soft hands and pretty dresses, ever agreeing to be a farmer's wife. Never even intended to ask her. That's how sure I was. I loved her something fierce, but I thought we couldn't make our lives fit together."

"You never told me that."

"Of course not, because you see how it all worked out. Turns out, your mama can handle a farm kitchen just fine, and I can put on a starched shirt every once in a while. There are other places where we've needed to bend, but neither of us broke. The important thing for you here, Faith, is to recognize that's not the place where we started. That's where we ended up. If you'd have asked me thirty-five years ago, I would have told you it was impossible. I couldn't see any other way." His blue eyes meet my matching ones. "Give it a little time. I know you think you need to rush, but he has to see how to bend and so do you."

I'm not sure this is something that Cade's going to compromise on, but I don't tell my father this. He doesn't know Cade the way I do. Still, if my father and mother were able to find a way to make things work, maybe there's *hope* for me and Cade after all.

"I'm finished here. Make sure to come and say hello to your mother when you're done." He dusts his hands on the front of his faded work jeans. "And maybe give Cade a minute to think. Cut the boy some slack." He winks at me, and I roll my eyes. "Not everybody can get it right all the time. Not everyone can be like your father."

This time I roll my eyes so hard I'm afraid they'll stick.

## 44

*Cade*

"Damn it." The stapler makes a satisfying *thwack* when it hits the wall, but it doesn't make me feel any better. I'm looking around for something else to throw when Charlie pokes his head into my office.

"Everything okay in here?"

I glare at him. "Obviously not, asshole."

"Whoa, calm down. No need for the profanity."

"Don't lecture me." I stand up and retrieve my broken stapler from the floor. "I can call an asshole an asshole if I want to."

"That's very mature. Seriously, if you keep throwing things in here, Chance is going to have your hide. I think you put a dent in the wall with that fast ball." He makes the mistake of coming all the way in and running his hand along the spot where my stapler made contact. "Yep, there's a place here, all right."

"There's about to be one in your skull if you don't get out of my office." I'm still holding the stapler, and Charlie has the good sense not to turn his back on me.

"I was hoping we could talk."

"I don't have time right now. Besides, what's there to say? I think we both know where we stand." Charlie wants me to apologize for breaking his trust, but that would mean saying it was wrong to have been with Faith. I can't bring myself to even think that, much less say it.

"What's so important you can't make time for your brother?" Charlie smirks, and I once again consider braining him with the stapler.

"Well, in addition to all the things happening with our festival, Sadie Mae's, and Stolen Barn Spirits, the mill sale has gone belly up." I let my head fall forward, hoping to loosen some of the stress there. It doesn't work. "So, if you could get the hell out of here so I can work, I'd appreciate it."

"The Cutters aren't going to sell you the mill?"

"Nope. They can get more money from a developer who wants to build another stupid subdivision. All Sammy sees is dollar signs." I look at the stack of papers on my desk. All these attempts to come up with a solution and not a one of them worth a flip. "Faith's not happy."

"Word on the street is she's unhappy about more than just the mill, little brother."

I scowl. "Screw you, Charlie."

"Oh, come on." Charlie throws his hands up. "You did exactly what I told you not to do. You got mixed up with Faith and she got hurt. I hope it was worth it, because while you thought you were just having a good time, she thought it was something real."

"It is—it *was* something real," I argue, my blood already heating up at the accusation.

"Then why would you end it the way you did, Cade?" It's a valid question, and Charlie's going to wait for an answer.

"Look, not that it's any of your business, but I ended it for her own good. Faith wants things I can't give her, and eventually she would have figured that out." I go back to the papers on my desk. "You can shut the door on your way out."

"Oh, I'm not going anywhere, not after a half-assed answer like that. What does Faith want that you can't give her? She's the easiest woman on the planet. What, she wanted you to promise you'd eat Brussels sprouts? Wash the tractor every week? What in the world did she want that you can't bring yourself to give her?" Charlie's angry eyes bore into me.

"She wants happily ever after, Charlie. She wants forever." The words burn like whiskey.

Charlie blinks. "You don't want her forever? Is that what you're saying? Because I should come over there and—"

"If you want to hit me, go on ahead and do it. It can't possibly hurt me any more than I'm already hurting." I hang my head. "I knew better, but I did it anyway."

"I don't understand. You don't want to get serious with Faith? Because for someone who just cut her loose on purpose you seem more conflicted than you should."

"You should know as well as anyone that I'm never going to settle down. Faith's like nobody else in the world—she's kind and thoughtful and beautiful, smart and funny and sexy."

Charlie's face wrinkles like he's smelled something awful.

"I know you see her like a sister, but I've never seen her like that. I love her, Charlie. I'm in love with her." My heart aches to say those words to Faith, but instead I'm telling my brother. That sounds about right, actually, given what I know about how love works.

"Did you tell her that?"

"Of course not. It wouldn't be fair to say those things when I know I can't commit. It would be cruel to start something I know is going to end." I shake my head. "I wouldn't do that to her."

"First of all, you did do that, genius. And second of all, why would you think you know how it's going to end? Do you have cancer or something?" Charlie takes a few steps forward and plants his butt in one of my leather chairs. "You're not psychic, little brother. No one knows the future."

"I know enough about relationships to know they always end." Charlie can't dispute that. I dare him to try.

"Why would you think that? I'm looking around this farm and seeing nothing but love in the air. Well, except between me and you right now." He smiles, but I don't smile back. This isn't a joke, and I'm not about to laugh.

"This minute, maybe, everyone's in love, but do you really think that's how things are going to go? For Cooper and Hadley? For Chance and Lily? For you and Jenna? How can you look at our parents and have any certainty about anything other than the probability of hating each other in the end?"

"Wow." Charlie leans back like he's been attacked by a strong gust of wind. "That's what this is about? Mom and Dad? Cade, they never should have gotten married in the first place, and barring that, they should have called it quits long before they did. You can't think they're a good example."

"They're the best example I know. They started out in love and ended up despising each other. Plenty of people do. Statistically, that's how it goes, Charlie. The divorce rate is still high. People still get hurt. I don't want Faith to end up like Mom."

"Cade." Charlie's bewildered face searches mine. "Faith isn't Mom, and you aren't Dad. You'd never treat her like that, and she'd never let you. That's what this is about?"

"I'm sure Mom never thought she'd ever end up where she is now, either."

Charlie sighs. "That's probably true, but I'd be willing to bet she'd still say she'd do it all over again. Well, maybe not all of it, but some of it."

I scoff. "I doubt that."

"You think she'd say she wished we'd never been born? You think she doesn't have fond memories of at least something?"

That stops me. I'd hate for my mother to wish I'd never been born, but I'd understand her wanting to forget she'd ever met my father. Avoiding that heartache would have to be tempting. That's what I'm doing for Faith—the thing my father should have done for my mother. The thing my mother couldn't do for herself. "If there's even the slightest chance I'd break Faith's heart like that, I'm not going to risk it."

"Look, I know you think you've got this all sorted out, Cade, but take it from me, she might think that risk would be worth taking. You can't protect her from getting hurt, no matter what you do. She doesn't want or need people to do that for her. Trust me, I've been trying for years." Charlie shrugs, settling back in the leather of the chair.

"How can you say that after the past few weeks? I've watched you screw things up with Jenna, seen the way you suffered." It's like Charlie doesn't remember the misery he went through.

"Oh, I suffered alright, and I deserved it. But look at me now. All that's in the past, Cade, and I'm happier than I've ever been."

I start to open my mouth to point out that Charlie might have to go through all that again, but he raises a hand to stop me.

"I know, I know—I can't say it's going to last forever, and you're right, but the way I feel right now is worth whatever might come in the future. And it sure beats sitting at home with a belly full of regret. I'd always be thinking about the what-ifs and the could-have-beens if I didn't put my heart on the line now. Besides, I'd have to guess the way you're feeling now's not exactly easy. You and Faith are still both suffering."

"You think I'm going to regret not trying?"

Charlie gives me a sad smile. "I know you are. You don't have to decide to have a bunch of babies this minute, Cade. You can take it slow. Just don't reject the idea out of hand. Faith's pretty great—you said so yourself—and you both deserve to be happy, even if I still should punch you in the mouth for going behind my back to do it."

"It wasn't too hard to do, actually. You were pretty distracted." I give Charlie a disappointed look of my own.

"I know. I've been an absentee friend here for a bit, but I'm going to make that up to Faith. I promise. You just promise me you'll tell her how you feel. All those fears are going to make you lose something really special."

I nod. "I'll think about it."

"You do that. In the meantime, I have an idea that might win us both a few get-out-of-the-doghouse points with your girl."

*My girl.* Charlie slides that in there like it's no big deal, but it makes my chest swell a bit. I'd like Faith to be my girl, if I haven't ruined everything. If it isn't too late.

"I've got an idea for saving this mill project. We'll need Cooper and Chance, but I think we can convince them."

Charlie's equal parts excitement and mischief, but I decide to trust him. He's turning out to be a little smarter than I would have given him credit for.

"Let's hear it then, because I'm all out of ideas."

And we get to work saving the day.

When my phone rings as I'm making myself a sad dinner for one, I think about not even bothering to see who's calling. There's really only one person I want to talk to and I'm sure she's not on the other end of the line. My house feels empty, suddenly far too big for just me, and any hope of changing that went out the door when Faith walked away from me. *For her own good*, I remind myself as I fumble around with my cell phone.

My blood runs cold when I see my mother's number lighting up the screen. "Mama, is everything okay?" She never calls me out of the blue and never at night.

"Well, you tell me, Cade. I just got a very interesting call. Something about you throwing away your chance to be happy with that adorable Baker girl."

*Charlie.*

I grit my teeth. "It wouldn't have worked out in the end."

"Why in the world would you say that? I saw the way the two of you look at each other." She seems genuinely perplexed.

"You know as well as I do that it doesn't matter how we feel *now*. All that can change, and I'm not risking Faith like that. I'm not going to be reckless with her the way Dad was with you."

"Oh, Cade." My mother's voice is small. "You can't go around living your life using my failed marriage as a road map for anything. Yes, your father was reckless—with me, with you boys—but you're not cut from the same cloth as him. I know you saw the worst of it, and maybe I should have tried to protect you a little better from my own suffering, but you aren't doomed to make the same mistakes."

"Statistically, there's a high likelihood things wouldn't have worked out for me and Faith. That's got nothing to do with you and Dad. That's facts." She can't argue with that. There's no blame there, no emotion. People get divorced, they break up. "It's better not to let things get to the point where she gets hurt."

"So you're protecting her, are you?"

"Of course I am. She's the most important thing, Mama."

"I guess I can't argue with your statistics or whatever, but I can tell you one thing for sure right now, and that's that your father has never once in his life said someone else was the most important thing. Already you're head and shoulders above where he was at your age—heck, where he is now—and you should be proud that you're unselfish. That said, I still think you're making a mistake." Her voice is firm and I know I'm not going to get far if I try arguing with her.

"I appreciate that, but you have to understand—"

"Oh, I understand. The scars you're carrying around from the divorce are deep and they're painful, it hurt you in a way it didn't hurt your brothers. But closing yourself off from even the possibility of getting the life you want is going to be just as painful in the long run."

"But if you had known how things were going to turn out, wouldn't you have done things differently? Wouldn't you have taken one look at Jeff Allen and run in the opposite direction?" I pace back and forth behind the island in my kitchen, letting the onion I've got sautéing on the stove start to stick and burn.

"Maybe, but most likely I would have gone on to make the exact same mistakes. And I don't regret the four fine boys I ended up with. I don't regret that one bit. I'm sure you and Faith will have your share of ups and downs, but you can't be afraid to live your life. You can't be worried about all the bad things that *might* happen. That paralyzes you, Cade, and you miss out on everything that could have been so good. Don't do that. That would be such a waste." I can almost hear her shaking her head through the phone line.

"But how do I get past the fear?" I nearly whisper it. I don't take chances, I always look before I leap. It goes against my nature to ignore the warnings that are so blatantly obvious.

"Do you love her?"

It's a simple question and one I don't even have to think about. "Of course I do."

"Then you just concentrate on that, Cade. Ignore everything else."

It seems too simple, too easy, and I'm not sure I can do it. Love can't possibly be enough, not to overcome the odds, not to convince Faith to give me another shot. "You think I can get her back?"

My mother laughs and the sound makes me smile in spite of myself. "You won't know until you try, Cade, but I'm confident you can convince her. It doesn't need to be a Power Point presentation, just speak from the heart."

"Thanks for the advice, Mama." I'm still going to kill Charlie for making her worry, but talking to my mother like this has been good. I feel lighter somehow. I've still got a lot to fix with Faith, but maybe it's not as impossible as I'd thought.

"Of course. You let me know when I can come for a visit and meet your girlfriend."

"You seem pretty sure she's going to forgive me." I can only hope my mother's right.

"How could she not, Cade? All that Allen charm and that handsome face? Plus, I'm sure your groveling is going to be exceptional. You just listen to your mama and everything should turn out fine." I can hear her smile and it makes me smile, too.

"Yes, ma'am."

Time to plan some exceptional groveling.

## 45

*Faith*

"I could have sworn we decided no clowns."

"Is there a clown? I don't see one." Molly pretends to scan the horizon.

"Right there. Making balloon animals. The guy with the bright orange wig and giant shoes?" I point to the clown in question.

"Oh, now I see him," Molly feigns surprise. "I'll have to ask around about that. Those balloon animals sure are cute, though."

I purse my lips and try to keep from rolling my eyes. "How's everything else?" I've been putting fires out all morning, but it looks like the festival is gearing up to be a good time.

"Everyone's checked in for the booths. People went all out. I'm hoping we get a good crowd, because there are some really wonderful things for sale. Next year we won't have any trouble getting companies to participate if the turnout today is what we expect."

The tables we've set up for the vendors do look amazing.

We've got a few local farms in addition to Happy Trails, plenty of local artisans and craftsmen, and local restaurants, too. Sadie Mae's is doing the bulk of the food, but we all agreed making this a true community event would attract more interest. And money. Even though that won't go to the mill, I'm trying to come to terms with it. Molly and I are already looking into other sites. Mint Springs has history to spare once you start digging around. Cutter's Mill still has a special place in my heart, but if it's going to end up a subdivision, at least I know we tried our best.

"Keep your fingers crossed the weather holds." I look up at the sky. There's a chance of thunderstorms today, but I'm hopeful they'll pass us by.

"If it doesn't, we can move most of it inside, I think. This space is amazing." Molly gives an excited twirl of her index finger. "I still can't believe Cade and his family are letting us use it for free."

The new events barn is pretty incredible. Between the open air pavilion and the fancy new barn structure, we have plenty of space. There are fairy lights already hung in preparation for tonight. I can easily imagine beautiful weddings out here. I get that little twinge in my heart again. Plenty of women will get to say "I do" to the loves of their lives out here, but not me. That's not even a distant possibility now.

"Make sure you thank him when you see him."

Molly furrows her brow. "Why don't *you* thank him?"

"Because I'm most likely not going to talk to him. Besides, between the general festival stuff and the Happy Trails booth, I'll be busy." I'm one-hundred-percent professional. I won't have time to talk to Cade.

"Well, I also have general festival stuff and my own booth. I can't leave Brad in charge of Smock It to Me all day. I think you might have to be the one who talks to Cade."

"Talk to me about what?"

I jump. He's close enough for me to get a whiff of the familiar scent of his skin, and my body betrays me, lighting up all over. "Making sure to thank you for letting the Historical Society use this place." I take two steps back to put some space between us.

"No need to thank me. I'm one of the founding members of the Historical Society, after all." He gives us a big smile. "Faith, can I talk to you for a second?"

"I'm pretty busy. I was actually on my way to make sure the Happy Trails booth was ready to go." I don't wait for Cade to say anything else; I turn on my heel and walk away. I hear him call after me, but I ignore him, speed-walking to the safety of my family farm's booth and the comfort of my vegetables.

Or *relative* safety and comfort, because my sisters are all there helping. Today looks to be a busy day, and my father can't run the whole show himself, so Charity, Hope, and Constance have been roped into reluctant service.

"Did I just see you run away from Cade Allen?" Of course Connie was watching.

"I wasn't running." I get three exasperated stares. "I was hurrying back over here to make sure we were all set up."

"We are fine. We arranged everything just the way you wanted. You can check our work," Hope tells me with a bossy hand on her hip.

"I'm going to." I can already see they've done a fine job, but I'm going to be hanging out here as long as humanly possible. There's no way Cade'll come over here if he thinks he'll have to deal with my nosy, gossipy sisters. If he values his privacy, he'll keep his distance.

"I really only need a minute." Cade's obviously got a death wish.

"I don't have a minute to spare." I shrug and go back to counting the cucumbers.

"Not even for me?" There's the tiniest bit of hurt in his voice.

All of my sisters hear the question, and all three visibly lean closer to hear my answer.

"No, Cade, not even for you." I'm not going to let him get under my skin again. "Sorry, but I need to get to work."

He stands there for a minute more, waiting for me to change my mind, and each second is excruciating. I keep my back to him and try not to hyperventilate. I've spent the time since the night of the party trying to get over him; it hasn't come close to working, but at least I can fake it a little. If I'm not looking at him and he's not breathing down my neck, that is. He's doing both now, and I'm coming undone. I'm having a time keeping my hands pressed to my sides—they only want to reach for him.

Finally, he walks away, and I breathe a sigh of relief. My sisters, however, aren't letting me off that easily.

"*Did you turn him away*? Faith, are you an idiot?"

Hope isn't the only one who thinks I'm making a mistake, according to the expressions on my other sisters' faces.

"I'm not an idiot, Hope. I'm trying to keep a little of my dignity." I square my shoulders and wish I could feel as confident as I sound.

"From where I'm sitting, it looked like maybe he was going to grovel a little," Charity offers and the others nod their heads.

"He's made it clear where he stands." No matter how hard it is for me to accept.

I spend the day running from Cade. He's everywhere, and whenever I think I've escaped him, he pops up again, always trying to get my attention, always trying to get 'just five minutes.'" He's over by the funnel cake stand, next to the ring toss, cozying up to that stupid clown. I cannot avoid him, no matter how hard I try.

"Looks like you've been moving all day." My father's enjoying that caramel apple a little more than he should.

"This thing is a full-time job." I duck behind the table full of late season tomatoes.

"Seems like it." He crunches down on the apple again. "Lots of hiding, too," he says after he chews and swallows.

"I'm making sure we've got plenty of produce back here. Wouldn't want to run out of something." I pretend to shuffle the cardboard cartons around.

"Your sisters and I have that all under control. You've done a great job with this, Faith. Everyone I've talked to is impressed."

I poke my head up over the tabletop. "Thank you. Molly and I have been working our butts off."

"Cade, too, I reckon." He takes another bite of the infuriating apple.

"He's done his share."

"He was looking for you earlier." He tries to say it in that offhand way other people can pull off but my father never can.

"I've been busy."

He raises his eyebrows. "You're eventually going to have to talk to him, Faith."

"He can't possibly have anything to say that I want to hear."

"Well, we may be about to find that out." My father points toward the section of the pavilion where the bands have been playing. Only now, instead of guitars and fiddles, it's only Cade standing there, tapping his fingers on the microphone.

"If I could have everyone's attention, please. I have a few important announcements to make." He scans the crowd, and his eyes settle on me.

I gulp.

"I promise not to take too much of everyone's time. I have a few things to say that just can't wait." His eyes stay focused on my face, and my knees go a little weak. Whatever Cade's got to say, he's going to do it whether I like it or not.

## 46

*Cade*

I am sweating. Not a little glisten on the forehead, no. I'm nervous enough to have beads of sweat gathering all over me. I'm hoping no one notices that or the way my hands are shaking as I pull the microphone from its stand and start to speak. This was absolutely not my plan, coming up on the stage and demanding everyone's attention, but Faith left me no choice. If I want her to hear me out, I'm going to have to make her—and the entire town of Mints Springs along with her.

*Tap, tap, tap.*

"If I could have everyone's attention, please? I have a few important announcements to make." I find Faith in the crowd. She's at her family's vegetable booth, hiding behind a table full of tomatoes. *Here goes nothing.* "I promise not to take too much of everyone's time. I have a few things to say that just can't wait."

I haven't clued Molly in on what I'm about to do, and I can see her waving frantically from the corner of my eye. She's most likely planned her own way of thanking everyone for coming and announcing how much money we've raised. I'm stepping on her toes for sure, ruining her carefully choreographed moment. But I can't stop now, I have to keep talking or else I'll lose my nerve.

"First of all, thank you all for coming. I'm Cade Allen, and I'm a member of the Mint Springs Historical Society. I know Molly Eagan's going to get up here in a second with a much better speech about all the work that went into today and how thankful we are for everyone's donations, but I have a special announcement. As y'all know, this event today was supposed to be all about raising money toward saving Cutter's Mill. It's a special piece of history, and we were disappointed when we thought it was going to be sold to a developer instead of to us. I'm happy to report that's not the case. The Cutters have generously decided to donate the mill and the property around it to the Historical Society. All the money we raise today can go directly toward the renovations."

There's the expected applause along with a few gasps. When I look for Faith, she isn't where she was before. I frantically search the faces in front of me and come up empty. *Where the hell is Faith?*

I take a deep breath. "Making this all come together took a little bit of time and a whole lot of negotiation."

I look out at the back of the pavilion and see all of my brothers there, arms folded over their chests. They know what I need to do, and from the looks of it, I'm not doing it right. Charlie motions with his hand for me to speed it up. *Get to the point*, he mouths, and I look again for Faith. None of this is worth doing if she doesn't hear it.

"The thing is, I have more than one announcement to make today. The Cutter family donating the mill is a wonderful thing to get to tell everyone after all the work everyone at the Historical Society put in. Molly and Faith and all the other committee members have done a great job."

Molly's standing near the edge of the stage, motioning for me to give her the microphone. I'm babbling, and she's not about to have her moment in the spotlight taken away by a bumbling idiot. I've probably got around thirty seconds before she snatches the mic out of my hand and pushes me back out into the crowd.

And it's a crowd now. More people have come to the pavilion from the barn, and the festival goers who had been playing the carnival games have stopped all the whooping and hollering. I get the sensation that I might throw up—my stomach is ready to revolt against this public display any second now.

"But the main thing I need to say today—Faith? Where is Faith Baker?"

Plenty of people are ready to help me locate Faith, who's apparently been hiding in the back of the crowd. Debbie from Ham & Eggs gives her a little push toward the front, and Mr. Sims from the liquor store blocks her when she tries to make a quick retreat. She has no choice but to move closer and closer to me until we're standing only a few feet apart.

I look into Faith's eyes and try to get the courage to do what I need to do. In private, this would have been hard enough. Here, with all these eyes watching, it's damn near impossible. I clear my throat.

"Honestly, I never would have become a part of the Historical Society if it wasn't for Faith. I didn't have much interest in the history of Mint Springs...but I had plenty of interest in Faith." There are more than a few titters at this admission, but I push forward. "I've always had plenty of interest in Faith Baker."

I take another look at Faith. Her mouth is hanging open a little bit, her brow furrowed in confusion.

"And while I worked on a way to save Cutter's Mill because it's important to Mint Springs, I really worked as hard as I did because it was important to Faith. I didn't want to disappoint her, especially since I've done my fair share of that lately." I break eye contact with Faith and look down at my feet for a second. *Keep going, Cade, you don't get another shot.*

"The thing is, I tend to like facts and figures. I'm all about the data, and that makes me ignore the things other people rely on—feelings, emotions, all of that. I've been ignoring my feelings for so long now, I can't remember the last time I've followed my gut. If I'd been listening to that, I probably would have tried to kiss Faith a long, long time ago. Because I've got feelings for Faith Baker, and I'm letting everybody know. I'm crazy in love with Faith and have been since I was about nine years old."

I can hear a few chuckles from the audience, but I ignore those. The crowd's long since fallen away from my focus, and now it's just me and Faith. She's waiting for me to finish, the expression on her face one of both surprise and wonder.

"She gave me a chance, but I blew it. I didn't tell her how I felt, and I tried to do what I always do—I looked at the numbers. Love's a bad bet when you think about it that way. And I looked at the people around me, thinking I had everything figured out. The thing I didn't count on, though, is the way I feel about Faith." I shake my head. "There's no accounting for that kind of thing.

"But it has recently come to my attention that I may have

made some false assumptions, because being without Faith is way worse than I ever imagined, and I may have been wrong about the way the world works when it comes to matters of the heart. So I'm up here now asking you to forgive me, Faith. I was wrong to insist love isn't worth a little risk and a little pain. I need you, Faith, with all your silly jokes and looking on the bright side, with all your determination and strength. I might not deserve it, but I'd love the chance to prove that to you."

There are several sighs and the expected hollering from my brothers. I don't care about anyone's reaction but Faith's, though, and she isn't exactly rushing the stage to throw her arms around my neck. In fact, she's turning around and running out of the pavilion. It's about as close to a no as she can give me without actually saying anything. I stand there reeling for a second, feeling like I've taken a punch to the gut.

"Go after her!" The shout comes from over by the Happy Trails booth. "She's a fast runner, son, but your legs are longer." Faith's father smiles at his own little quip. "Go finish what you started."

You don't have to tell me twice.

## 47

*Faith*

The only thing I can think to do is run. I hear everything Cade's saying, but I know he can't really mean those things. They're pretty words—beautiful ones—that can't possibly be what he's feeling. He was serious when he told me he wasn't the kind to settle down, and I'd believed him. What's changed since then? Nothing.

"Faith!" A hand closes around my elbow. "Wait."

Of course Cade came after me. He's just declared his undying love for me and I took off like a rabbit caught in the cabbage patch. My heart's still pounding in my chest, and it doesn't slow down when Cade spins me around to face him. His eyes search mine. Hot tears sting my cheeks as I try to look away. Cade releases me and takes two steps back.

"Why would you do that?" I demand. "You had to know doing that in front of everyone would be humiliating."

"I tried all day to talk to you in private, Faith. And if having me tell everyone I'm in love with you is *humiliating* then I don't know what to say." Cade shakes his head and runs his hands through his hair. "I thought you'd be happy that I've come around."

"Come around?" I hate the desperate way the words come flying out of my mouth. "Am I supposed to forget all the things you've said before? I can go along with plenty of things, Cade, but not you deluding yourself that you might be able to one day think about marriage and kids." I sound insane. He's giving me everything I said I wanted, and I'm throwing it back in his face.

"Can we calm down a little bit here?" Cade reaches for me again but then thinks better of it. "Here. Sit." He gestures to the fallen tree on the ground next to us. I've run directly into the pine forest, effectively hiding us from the crowd of the festival but making me hopelessly alone out here with Cade. "Come on, you know I don't bite."

His words make me shiver. I might be upset, but I still haven't forgotten how it feels to be close to Cade. I give in and put my backside on the log.

Cade sits down next to me, making sure we don't touch. "I thought you wanted me to be open to settling down."

I wipe my cheeks with the back of my hand. "I *did*... I *do*. But I don't want you to say that just because you think it's what I want to hear. That doesn't get us anywhere. I want to hear it if it's *real*." My tears start again, and I angrily brush them away. Faith Baker crying over a man again. Amazing.

"Faith." Cade reaches for my hand. "It *is* real. I meant everything I said back there. I wouldn't stand up in front of all of Mint Springs and lie. You know me better than that."

"But see, I do know you, and I know you meant what you said at Mae's party, too. Which one of those heartfelt speeches am I supposed to believe?" I glare at him, but keep my hand in his. The warmth of his palm still feels reassuring, despite the circumstances.

Cade looks away, but when his gaze returns to mine, it's fierce. "Both, in a way. Back at Mae's party I really did believe I was doing what was best for you by letting you go. That hurt, Faith, but I was doing what I thought would hurt less in the long run."

"But—"

"Let me finish." He gives my hand a squeeze. "I've had time to reconsider, and I've had people point out the error of my thinking. Now, I'm not saying I want to run off and get married today, and the idea of being responsible for a baby... Well, that still gives me heart palpitations, honestly, but I know it doesn't feel the way it did before. Thinking about those things with you, that's different. It isn't some data point or hypothetical; it's a real possibility."

"You just changed your mind?" It seems ridiculous that Cade would go from "absolutely not" to "a real possibility."

"*You* changed it. With a little help from Charlie, I guess." Cade's grin is sheepish. "Never thought I'd be giving him credit for something like that."

"Proof miracles do exist."

Cade laughs. "I guess so." He turns his body so our knees touch. "Faith, I'm not going to make promises I can't keep, but I can promise you I'm going to give this everything I have. Is that enough?"

*Is it?* I tilt my head back and look through the tops of the pine trees. *Is there really any more he could promise than that?*

"How'd you pull off that stunt with the mill?"

"It was hardly a stunt; it was good business." Cade puffs out his chest. "Doubt me in other areas all you want, but in business I know what I'm doing. Cooper, Chance, and Charlie helped me convince Sam Senior that what he really wanted wasn't a big chunk of cash. Turns out he didn't know what Sammy was planning. Didn't take much to get from there to donating the whole shebang."

"Really? I am impressed." I sneak a look at Cade's handsome profile when he looks back out through the trees.

"He said he felt like we understood family legacy, and he trusted us to do right by him." Cade's voice softens. "I want you to trust me again, Faith. Let me show you I can do right by you, too."

His words pull at my heart, turning all the stubbornness I've been feeling inside out. "Did you mean what you said about being in love with me?"

"Every single word. Nine-year-old me didn't know what hit him."

"I thought you never even noticed me at all."

Cade puts a dramatic hand to his heart. "Not noticed? That, Faith Baker, would have been impossible. Now, tell me you've been in love with me since elementary school, too, and we can get back to the festival. You know everyone's waiting."

He's joking, but little does he know. "What if I said you were right? That I've been in love with you since the first time I saw you jump your bicycle over the edge of the creek the summer after fourth grade?"

A giant smile lights up his face. "I'd say you were lying, but I know you better than that. And that bike maneuver is pretty sweet. You still feel that way?"

I nod, tears streaking my face for a different reason now.

"Then let's get back to this party." He stands, keeping a firm grip on my hand, and we walk back to the pavilion and a million questioning eyes. Only this time I don't mind at all because Cade's right by my side.

And he's going to stay.

# EPILOGUE

**Two years later**

*Cade*

"I thought we all agreed that this year there'd be no clowns."

Molly shrugs. "People love them, Faith. If we didn't have them, it would ruin the whole experience for everyone."

"The entire festival would be ruined without the clown? Oh, come on. The caramel apples? Maybe. The cake walk? Probably. But the clown? Absolutely not." Faith is adamant.

"You sure are cute when you get all riled up." I reach for her, and she lets me pull her close.

"The festival is serious business, Cade, and this year has to be extra special." She wrinkles her nose as I plant a kiss on it.

This is the first year we've been able to have the festival here at the mill. The renovations have taken a year longer than expected. Between raising the money we needed and discovering several structural issues with the buildings, we've been busy out here with seemingly nothing to show for it.

Until today.

The parking lot is full, and pretty much everyone in town has come out to take a look at the new and improved Cutter's Mill. Chance and his team outdid themselves, keeping things as true to the original buildings as possible while also making them functional and modern. We've got several teaching spaces and a little museum in the main building, and the old general store's been turned into a space for selling the work of local artisans. Starting next spring we'll be having a weekly farmers market led by Faith and her team at Happy Trails. Even the meadow's putting on a show, still full of wildflowers, even here in the first week of September. We talked about moving the event to later in the year so it could be a true harvest festival, but by now it's tradition. The first week of September means the first days of school and the Mint Springs Festival. Every year, forever and ever, amen.

"I have to hand it to you, little brother. This looks good." Charlie comes up next to me and slaps me on the back. "The turnout's great; Jenna's worried she's going to run out of tarts." He pulls Faith away from me and I growl. He's lucky I know he's madly in love with Jenna, otherwise there might be an Allen brothers wrestling match right about now.

"Cade's been busting his butt," Molly offers, smiling big in her monogrammed sweater. "We couldn't do it without him. Or the rest of you. We appreciate all the food and beverage donations again this year."

"We're happy to help. Sadie Mae's gets as much out of this event as we give, that's for sure." Charlie releases Faith and I take her right back into my arms. "Calm down, Cade. That is a serious level of PDA, bud."

"Jealous?" I ask him. I'm teasing, but I know he does love Faith, just not the way I do.

"Always. That's why you'd better take good care of that girl." He yells it as he walks backward away from me. He knows I've got big plans for today. No need to scold me about how I treat Faith. Charlie gives me a wink before he turns around, waving hello to everyone he sees along the way back to Jenna and the Sadie Mae's booth.

"We have to make sure we mention Chance in our speech today. He deserves to get a big round of applause." Molly makes a note on the piece of paper attached to her clipboard.

"What's this 'we' business?" Faith asks. "I think you're making the speech this year. When I did it last year it was a disaster."

"But the year before that..." Molly waggles her eyebrows. "It's hard to top that one."

"That one was exceptional." Faith kisses me on the cheek. "Now, if you'll excuse me, I have to go and make sure my sisters are at least pretending to sell vegetables."

I smile as she walks away from me. Faith in her overalls is still the hottest thing I've ever seen.

"Oh my gosh, she doesn't suspect a thing," Molly gushes. "She's going to pee her pants." She's almost jumping up and down with excitement.

"I hope not." I'm still not convinced Faith is going to be happy with the surprise I've got on tap for later today. Last time I spilled my guts in front of everyone it turned out okay, but there's no guarantee today will be the same. Peeing pants would not be on my list of good reactions.

"She's going to say yes. Don't you worry."

The ring's been burning a hole in my pocket all morning. I've had it hidden in the back of my sock drawer for months, because it's the one place I can be sure Faith doesn't poke around. Now that she's living with me, it's harder to orchestrate surprises. I might have acted like I wasn't sure about marriage and family, but once I got my head around it, it's all I've been thinking about. I've been planning this proposal since last spring, trying to keep from just blurting it all out and asking Faith every time I see her. Today, though, it might be Molly who spills the secret.

"When are you planning to ask her? During the speech? Should I give a signal? Wait, no. *You* give *me* a signal." Molly's talking a mile a minute.

"Don't worry about that. You don't have to do anything at all. When it's my turn, I'll take care of everything." If I don't throw up on my shoes, that is.

"Got it. T-minus two hours and counting." She pats me on the arm and then rushes off to take care of the million things that can go wrong on festival day.

Filling those next two hours is excruciating. I catch glimpses of Faith with various neighbors and friends, smiling that big smile of hers. I cannot wait to make her officially mine in front of everyone here. I'm basically twiddling my thumbs, walking around to make small talk and shake the hands of people all excited to congratulate me on the way the mill turned out. I eat a funnel cake that I start to regret the second Molly calls me up to the stage. That thing is threatening to make a repeat performance as I bide my time during her speech.

The Cutter family is here, Sammy shooting daggers at me with his eyes. He's never quite gotten over the fact that I was able to convince his grandfather to give us the mill. Even though his real estate business is booming in part because his family is seen as heroes for the donation, he still blames me for keeping him from his early retirement. But not even that can dampen my spirits as I stand on the makeshift stage we've got set up next to the water wheel and the stream.

"Cade, would you like to say a few words?" Molly gives my arm an aggressive squeeze.

"Thank you, Molly." The timing on this is crucial, and my hired helper doesn't miss his cue. Before anyone else can say a word, our clown friend approaches the stage and honks one of those obnoxious air horns.

"What the heck?" Faith recoils a bit at the intrusion of a pair of floppy shoes and that fake red nose.

The clown's holding a half-finished balloon animal and he gets right to work completing it as he comes to stand next to Faith. She's trying not to lose her cool, but he keeps invading her space. He's hard at work on his balloon, and once it's complete, he tries to hand it to Faith.

"No, thank you." Faith refuses his gift, not noticing what everyone else in the crowd has already figured out. It's not an animal at all, but a giant ring. When she turns away from the clown, I'm down on one knee.

Faith startles, accidentally taking the balloon engagement ring from her clown nemesis.

"What are you doing?" she whisper-hisses at me.

"Exactly what it looks like I'm doing." I give one more nervous look to the crowd and then focus my attention on my girl. "Faith, I've loved you since the first time I saw you, and these past few years that love has only grown. You've taught me how to really live life and shown me a version of the future I can't wait to start with you. You're everything I could possibly want. Faith Baker, would you make me the happiest man in the world and agree to be my wife?"

Faith's expression isn't the kind you see in movies where the heroine enthusiastically says yes to the proposal. Her eyes narrow as she looks down at me, still holding the balloon ring in one hand, the other coming to rest on her hip. "Are you serious?"

"Um, yes." I can feel the eyes of the entire town bearing down on me.

"You bought a ring and everything?" She squints down at the object in my outstretched hand.

"Yes. One you don't have to take off to work on the farm. The diamond's set low, see? But if you don't like it, we can get something else." This wasn't the conversation I thought we'd be having up here on the stage. Maybe I've misinterpreted what Faith wants. Maybe she's going to say no.

Luckily, she puts me out of my misery.

She gets down on her knees too and kisses me full on the mouth. "Of course I'll marry you, Cade. Just wanted to make you sweat a little bit."

I slip the ring on her finger and kiss her again as the crowd erupts into cheers. I can hear my brothers yelling the loudest despite the general mayhem. "I thought you were going to say no," I whisper into her ear.

"How could I say no?" she whispers back. "But I had to make you work a little after that thing with the clown." She shudders.

I tilt my head back and laugh. "I love you, Faith."

"And I love you right back."

Yeah, I think Faith and I are going to do just fine. I'm going to make every second count.

. It's a reverse age gap romance with plenty of steam.

# ACKNOWLEDGMENTS

Thank you all for reading *Make It Count*. Book four took longer than expected, but Cade and Faith finally started talking. I hope you loved their story and enjoyed taking another visit to Mint Springs.

Thank you to my editor, Kiezha Ferrell. I had some deadline trouble with this one, and she did her best not to strangle me even though I'm sure she wanted to. Thank you for working around my slow pace this time around.

Thank you to Austin Ryan for her proofreading work and all the final tweaking. I know if Austin likes it, then y'all will too. She's one of my biggest cheerleaders and I appreciate that so, so much.

Thank you to Kate Farlow for another beautiful cover. She's got a much better eye than I do and she can make an image sing. Cade and Faith's book is better for it.

And, thanks to my kids. They take these books as seriously as I do. From my oldest repping my titles at his local college bar (ahem...college? How did that happen?) to my youngest helping to write the punniest blurbs around, they've got my back. My middle one's the queen of story arc so I've got the dream team over here, folks. Love you three to the moon and back.

# ABOUT THE AUTHOR

Jessie Harper writes steamy, contemporary romance with a slightly Southern flavor. Originally from Nashville, Tennessee, she has lived all over the world—from Europe to Asia. She currently resides in Park City, Utah with her husband, three children, and more rescue animals than she ever intended. She appreciates a nice glass of whiskey, homegrown tomatoes, and well-delivered sarcasm. She hopes to never have to "bless your heart."

For updates and more visit www.jessieharper.com. Or sign up for Jessie's newsletter so you never miss a thing.

facebook.com/JessieHarperAuthor
twitter.com/jessiehromance
instagram.com/jessieharperromance
bookbub.com/authors/jessie-harper
amazon.com/Jessie-Harper/e/B089PV285Y